Also available from Abigail Strom

Almost Like Love

Nothing Like Love

Anything But Love

The Landry family series:

The Millionaire's Wish

Cross My Heart

Waiting for You

Into Your Arms

The Hart University series:

Rikki (Freshman Year)

Claire (Sophomore Year)

Tamsin (Junior year - coming soon)

Julia (Senior year - coming soon)

CLAIRE

HART UNIVERSITY, BOOK 2

Abigail Strom

Cover Art © Sarah Hansen, Okay Creations
Book Layout © BookDesignTemplates.com

Claire: Hart University, Book 2/ Abigail Strom.
ISBN 978-1943296033

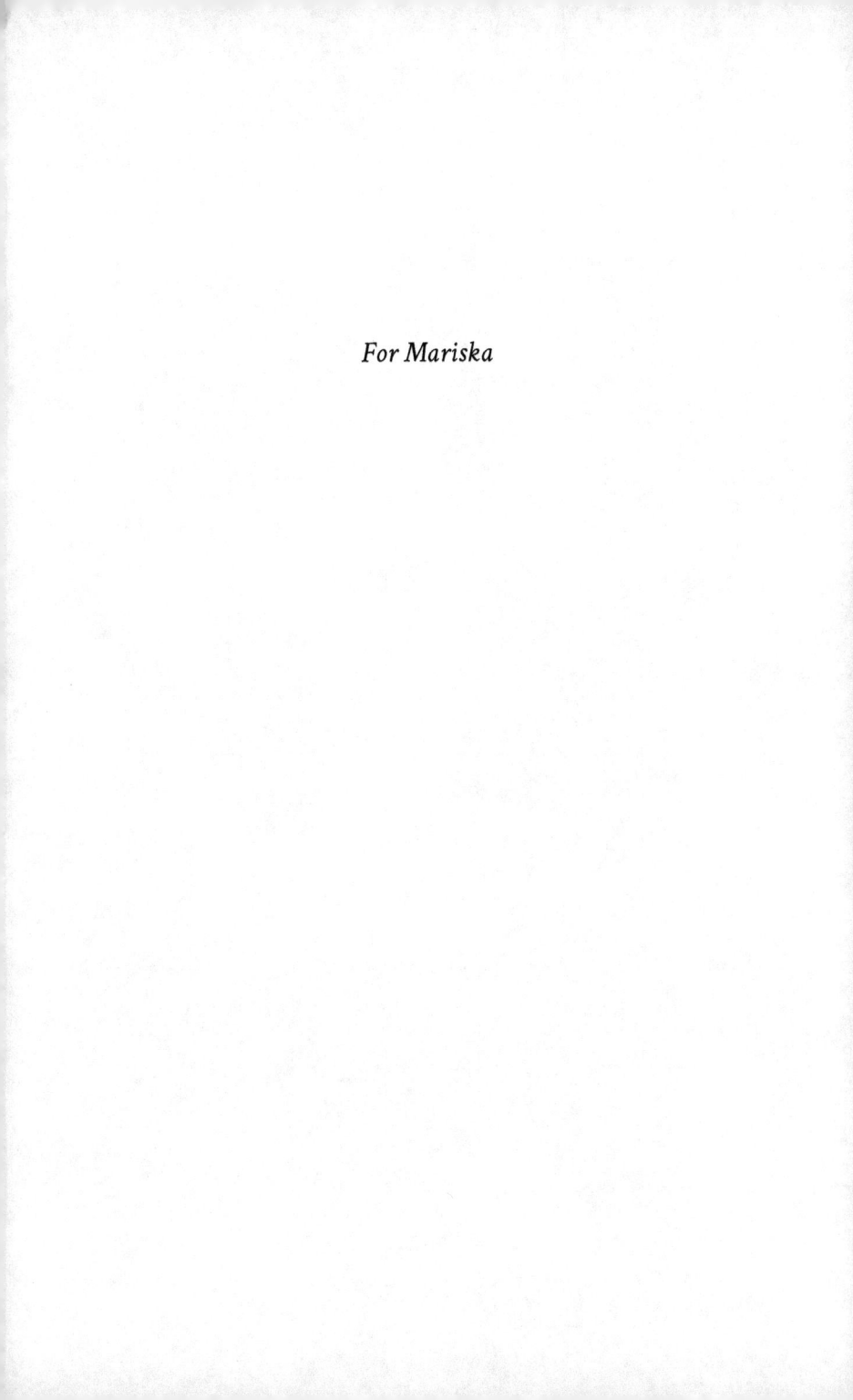

For Mariska

My freshman year at Hart University started with me staring across a room at Claire Stone.

Okay, so, that's not technically accurate. Other things happened first. Moving into my dorm, meeting my roommate . . . not to mention preseason football training camp. Important things.

But the first time I saw Claire felt like the beginning of everything.

And now, sophomore year was starting off exactly the same way.

Last year it was the dining hall in Claire's dorm. This year, it was the big off-campus house I'd rented with some teammates.

We were throwing a back-to-school party and the place was packed. I'd broken up with my girlfriend back in June, but this was the first time I really felt single. I was trying to enjoy the feeling when I caught sight of Claire.

The moment I saw her, everything else went away. The noise, the heat, the hundreds of soon-to-be drunk college students—all of it.

My mother made me sit through *West Side Story* once. There were actually some pretty cool parts of the movie—the gang war between the Sharks and Jets, mostly—but there was one scene I couldn't have cared less about: the scene where Tony and Maria meet for the first time. It's at a dance, and when they see each other across the room, everything changes. The music slows down, all the other people fade into the background, and it's just the two of them.

I made puking sounds when I watched that scene with my mom. Because until I saw Claire for the first time, I thought love at first sight was a load of crap.

Now I knew better.

It wasn't just because she was gorgeous. I mean, she was . . . but there were girls here tonight some guys would think were hotter.

But it wasn't the fact that she was a beautiful girl that got me. It was the fact that she was *my* girl.

Of course at the time I'd had that realization, we were both seeing other people—which made me officially nuts. Not only was Claire not my girl, but I already had a girl. A girl I loved.

I convinced myself that my stupid crush on Claire was some away-from-home-and-my-girlfriend thing and that it would go away over time. I texted Lissa every day and sent jewelry for her birthday and Valentine's and felt like an asshole for thinking about another girl.

I saw Lissa back home in Ohio during winter break and after the school year was over. When she broke up with me in June, my biggest reaction was relief. I was pretty sure that also made me an asshole, or at least a really shitty boyfriend. I wasn't even mad that she'd cheated on me with another guy, because I felt like I'd cheated on her all year . . . even though it was only in my head.

Every time I saw Claire my stupid fucking heart went out of control. And at night when I got myself off, it was Claire I fantasized about.

And now I was seeing her in person for the first time in three months.

Her hair was a little different. It was the same shade of blond, but she'd had bangs last year and she'd grown them out over the summer.

She still wore her signature hat—a white fedora with a black band. And she had the same body—the body I'd seen in my dreams a hundred times. The body that made me wake up sweating in the middle of the night.

For the first time that day I was grateful for the August heat, because Claire was wearing a tiny camisole top and cutoff denim shorts. There was hardly anything between my eyes and her bare skin. My palms itched as I imagined covering her breasts with my hands and then sliding them down to her curvy hips . . . and pulling her close as I cupped that perfect ass.

She must have just come in, because she was standing near the front door scanning the room. I was a little surprised to see her here, because this was definitely not her crowd. She preferred to party with the creative types who lived in Bracton—the Hart U dorm for students interested in the arts.

Then she saw me, and her face lit up with this huge smile—and I swear to God my knees went weak.

She started across the room toward me and I stood there like an idiot, just waiting. Was it possible she'd come here tonight looking for me?

I hadn't seen Claire since the end of freshman year. A lot can happen over the summer, right? After all, she didn't know I'd broken up with my girlfriend. Maybe she'd broken up with her boyfriend.

Maybe we were both single.

"Check out little miss hotness coming this way. Who the hell is she and where has she been all my life?"

"Shut up, Delford."

I'd opened my mouth to say those exact words, but it wasn't me who said them—it was Andre. I'd been so focused on Claire I hadn't noticed that he and Delford were standing behind me in the keg line.

"That's a friend of mine, and I'd like to keep it that way," Andre said. "So keep your mouth shut, D."

Delford was working on his response when Claire reached us. She hugged Andre hello, and I had just enough time to wonder if she would hug me, too, when she did.

"Wow, it's so good to see you guys. How was your summer? When did you get back?"

It was a good thing Andre was there to answer her, because I needed a minute to recover from the hug.

For a good three seconds her body had been pressed up against mine. She was six inches shorter than me, but she'd gone up on her toes when she threw her arms around my neck and her breasts had been smushed up against my chest. She wasn't wearing perfume but she smelled amazing . . . clean and sweet, like she'd taken a shower just before coming out tonight.

Then she smacked me on the arm.

"What?" I asked.

"She asked you a question, man." That was Andre, who was grinning in a way that meant a shitload of mockery would be coming at me later on.

Before I could ask her to repeat it Delford stepped up.

Enter asshole, stage left.

"What do you say I show you around the place, sweetheart? Like say the bedrooms upstairs?"

I've never gotten so hot so fast. I think I would have punched him in the face if Andre hadn't grabbed my arm.

"Claire's got this, man," he muttered.

Claire was looking at Delford with her eyebrows up. "What's this about?" she asked, gesturing at his T-shirt.

I hadn't noticed what he was wearing until now—a white tee with the words "Get off my back and . . ." emblazoned on it. Then Delford turned around to show us the rest: ". . . get on yours."

Andre grabbed my arm again.

"Get off my back and get on yours," Claire repeated. "Wow, that's awesome. You're going to have girls falling all over you tonight." She shook her head slowly. "You know the message you're sending with that shit? You're saying to the world, I have a small dick and I'm bad in bed, so here's me overcompensating. Good luck with that."

Delford started to say something, but Andre hauled him out of the keg line and shoved him toward the stairs.

"Change that shirt and you can come back to the party," he said. Delford looked for a moment like he was ready to argue the point, but Andre—a guy slow to anger but absolutely not someone to mess with—was staring him down.

They stayed like that for a few beats. Then Del held up his middle finger, but he also went upstairs.

"Impressive crowd you guys are hanging with these days," Claire said. "I can totally see why you decided to get a house with a bunch of football players."

"We're football players, too," I reminded her.

"Yeah, that's something to brag about."

"Come on, Claire. You know they're not all like Delford."

"Sure," Andre said with a grin. "Some of them are like us."

Claire punched him on the shoulder, but she also started to laugh. And as the two of them started to joke around, I wondered why I couldn't be like Andre. Why I couldn't handle Delford without hitting him and make Claire laugh a minute later.

"So what's up with you and whatshisname?" I asked abruptly.

Claire and Andre stopped talking and stared at me.

"Your boyfriend," I clarified, feeling like an idiot. "Are you guys still together?"

Andre would have found some smooth, casual way to get that information. Me, I asked a question with all the subtlety of a sledgehammer.

"Yes," Claire said after a moment. "I'm still with whatshisname." She paused. "He's in town for a visit, actually. He's coming by later to hear the band."

Disappointment washed over me, followed by confusion. "The band?"

She stared at me. "Yes. We're playing your party tonight. Didn't you know?"

"I thought we hired a group called Sugar Lane?"

"That's us."

"It is?"

"You know we got a new lead guitarist, right? Well, last week we gave ourselves a new name."

"Oh," I said—the kind of brilliant response that captured my intellectual range when I was around Claire.

Claire took off her fedora, combed her hair back with her free hand, and put the hat back on. "Which reminds me—I'd better go help with the equipment. Where should we set up?"

"I'll show you," Andre said.

"Aren't you in line for beer?"

"I'll grab one later."

And just like that, Andre was walking with Claire over to the part of the living room we'd cleared out for the band—and I was left standing in the keg line.

"Here you go," someone said, and a red cup was shoved into my hand. I chugged it down without moving and tossed the empty into the big trashcan we'd put by the fridge.

"Give me another," I said, and I chugged that one, too. Only after my third did I give up my spot, heading out to the living room to look for Claire again.

Because even though she was still with her boyfriend, even though she was at this party because of a gig and not because of me, I still wanted to be around her. I still wanted to be where I could see her.

I parked myself on the beat-up couch against the wall where I'd have a view of the band.

"This year is about football, Will."

The couch sagged under Andre's weight as he sat down next to me.

"Huh?" I asked.

"You were QB3 last year and didn't take a single snap. This year you're in line for the top spot—if you focus."

"I'm focused."

"I'm not saying forget about girls. In fact I'm saying the opposite. You want to play loose in games, right? That means having fun when you're off the field. So have fun."

"I'm having fun. I'm having tons of fun."

"There are probably fifty girls here tonight who'd be thrilled to go out with you—or to hook up with you. So there's no reason to waste your time on a girl you can't have."

I did not want to have this conversation.

"Do me a favor, man."

"Yeah?"

"Shut the hell up."

Andre grinned. "I can't help it. You're like a cute little seal pup or something. I worry about you."

"The only place you should worry about me is on the field. You're a guard and that's your job. But off the field? I can take care of myself."

"If you say so."

"Is anyone else coming tonight?"

Andre stared at me. "What do you mean? A hundred people are here already and the party's barely started."

"I meant anyone else from Bracton."

Andre shrugged. "I don't know. I didn't ask those guys."

"Not even Dyshell?" Dyshell was his sister and Claire's roommate last year.

"Dyshell's still in Louisiana. She's coming back to-morrow."

"What about Rikki and Sam?"

"No. I mean, they know about the party, but I told them it wouldn't be their scene. It's kind of . . ." He hesi-tated. "I don't know, weird? To think of the Bracton crowd being here. Like two worlds colliding. Do you know what I mean?"

"Yeah." I knew exactly what he meant, and I was relieved he hadn't invited anyone else from that dorm. "That's why I kind of wish Claire wasn't here."

"That's different. She's in a band. It's her job to go wherever the gigs are." He paused. "I thought you knew she was in Sugar Lane when we hired them."

"Nope."

"Yeah, well, I'm sorry. I wouldn't have—I mean, if I'd known that you—"

He was veering closer to the topic I'd ruled out of bounds.

"Don't worry about it." I took a breath. "This is a party, damn it. Let's have a blast."

Andre nodded. "That's all I'm saying."

CHAPTER TWO

I don't know why it bugged me so much that one of Will McKenna's new housemates was a jerk. I mean, I knew Will and Andre played football. And while I didn't know much about the sport and hadn't been to a single game last year, I knew that some football players were, in fact, total douche bags.

It's a free country, and you're free to be a douche bag if that's what you want to do with your life. I just hated the idea that Will was hanging out with people like that.

Will was one of the sweetest guys I knew. With his reddish brown hair, green eyes, and killer bod, he was also smoking hot, but my relationship status meant that I couldn't pay any attention to that. Ted and I had been together since sophomore year of high school, and even though the long-distance thing was a little rocky, that didn't give me permission to drool over other guys.

This was the first time Ted had come to visit me in Massachusetts. He was pre-med at the University of Iowa, not far from our home town, so it had made more sense for me to visit him last year. We'd been together all summer, and I'd tried hard to be the perfect girlfriend to make up for the year we'd spent twelve hundred miles apart.

Maybe I'd tried too hard. Ted and I kept getting into fights no matter what I did, and when he announced that he was going to spend a week with me at Hart before he started his school year, I was so relieved he wasn't breaking up with me I'd almost cried.

The thing I was most excited about was the gig at the football party. Ted had seen me sing before but not with a band, and I wanted to share that part of my life with him. Maybe that would help us get back to the way we'd been in high school.

But in order for that magic to happen, he'd have to actually be here.

By the time the band was set up and ready to go, Ted still hadn't shown. I'd sent a bunch of texts with no response, and I was starting to worry.

I ducked outside where it was quieter and called Rikki.

"Hey, Claire. How's the gig?"

"It's just about to start. Could you do me a huge favor?"

"Sure."

When I'd left Bracton an hour ago, Ted had been in my room reading. I'd entered the lottery for a single this year so he and I could have privacy if he visited, and I'd been thrilled when I won—especially when he actually came to see me.

"Would you go down the hall to see if Ted's in my room? He's supposed to be here at the gig and he's not, and he's not answering his phone, either."

"No problem," Rikki said. "Hang on a sec."

A moment later I heard the sound of knocking followed by muffled voices. Then:

"Hey, Claire."

I was so surprised I almost dropped my phone. "Ted! Are you okay? What's wrong?"

"Nothing's wrong."

"But I thought you were coming to hear me play." I couldn't imagine what had happened, considering I'd given him detailed directions to the football house. "Did you forget how to get here?"

"No." There was a short silence. "To tell you the truth, I'm not really up for noise and crowds tonight. Do you mind?"

Did I *mind*?

I was so disappointed it felt like I'd been punched in the stomach. I didn't know what to say, so I focused on a detail.

"Why didn't you let me know? Or at least, you know, answer one of my texts?"

"I didn't hear the phone. It's probably dead. I'll charge it while you're out, okay?"

Ted's phone was *never* dead. He was always charging it. It was one of his obsessions.

But I couldn't get into a fight with him now. Rikki was there, for one thing—Ted was talking on her phone. And in five minutes I had to sing in front of a crowd. That meant I couldn't cry, because crying makes your voice sound like shit.

I took a deep breath. "Okay," I said. "Have a good night." Then I ended the call and stuck my phone in my pocket.

I went back inside to find Burns, our drummer, handing around a flask. "It's mezcal. Want a shot?"

I didn't usually drink before a gig, but I was willing to make an exception tonight.

"Yes," I said, taking the flask from Jocelyn when she was done. I tilted my head back and relished the burn of the alcohol, gulping down enough for a double. Then I handed it to Milton, our guitarist, who shook his head as he passed it back to Burns.

"I'm good."

"Okay, then," I said, looking around at the group. We'd been together a while but this was our first paying gig, and I would've felt nervous if my anxiety hadn't been swamped by pissed-off-ness. "Are we ready to go?"

Nods all around, and we took our positions—Milton on guitar, Jocelyn on bass, Burns on drums, and me at the microphone.

I'd been planning to do a short intro—our names, thanks for having us, we do a mix of covers and originals, hope you like it—but then I happened to see Will sitting on a couch over by the wall.

He wasn't alone. Two girls were draped all over him, and it looked like one of them had her tongue stuck in his ear.

I was so mad I started to shake. Of course it couldn't be Will I was mad at—he wasn't my boyfriend, so it shouldn't matter to me if he was flirting with a hundred girls. Ted was the one I was mad at, and I was just projecting it onto Will.

I was projecting so hard I wanted to kill him.

I went over to Burns. "Give me another shot," I said.

"I thought we were starting," he said, but he pulled the flask out of his pocket and handed it over.

I took a big gulp. "We are." I handed the flask back and wiped my mouth with the back of my hand. "Okay, here's the deal. I'm changing up the set list."

Milton started to object. "But we've been practicing those songs all week. Why would you—"

"I'm going with my gut, all right? I want to do our fuck-you set."

The fuck-you set was actually Milton's creation, put together last May when he broke up with his boyfriend.

Milton, Burns and Jocelyn all looked at each other, and then they looked at me.

"Okay here," Burns said.

"Yeah, okay," Jocelyn said.

We all looked at Milton, who brushed his thick bangs off his forehead and sighed. "Well, it's my set list. I'm fine with it. But tell me this before we start, Claire. Who are you pissed at?"

Ted. I'm pissed at Ted.

But then I looked over at Will, and saw that the cute brunette who'd been whispering in his ear was now in his lap, her arms around his neck and her tits in his face.

"Everyone," I said. Then I gripped the mic tighter and stepped forward. No one was paying attention yet, but I didn't care.

"Are you going to do an intro?" Milton asked.

"Nope." I took a breath and belted out, "One, two, three, *four!*"

We killed it.

I mean we absolutely *killed* it.

I belted out songs like I was Amy Winehouse, singing like every note might be my last. The set list we'd practiced for this gig was jock-friendly—created with the help of Andre, a football player as well as our former bassist—while our fuck-you set was more alt-and-indie rock friendly.

But the crowd ate it up.

I made eye contact with every guy in the room like I wanted to kill them or screw them, and I knew—I *knew*—I had them eating out of my hand.

I'd never felt like that before. This wasn't my style at all. I usually let my voice speak for me, not doing a lot of showy stuff on stage.

But tonight was different. Fueled by anger, I rocked out like my body was a lethal weapon, and when the crowd pressed close, dancing to the beat and shouting their approval between songs, I fed off their energy like it was a living thing—like we were all making something together, the four of us in the band and the people in the audience, creating electricity out of music and sweat and passion.

The one place I didn't look was over at the couch where Will had been. I didn't want to see him, didn't want to think about him. But during the last song before our break, I couldn't help seeing him. He was in the middle of the crowd with Andre beside him, and he was staring straight at me.

A fresh pulse of anger shot through my veins. Sweat was getting into my eyes and it stung, and that pissed me off too.

I pulled off my camisole top and used it to wipe the perspiration from my face, and when the audience howled I tossed my shirt to them, finishing the song in my pink satin bra.

Cheers filled the room when the set was done, and I caught my breath before telling the crowd, "We'll be back in a few. In the meantime, don't do anything I wouldn't do."

"Holy *shit!*" Jocelyn exulted as the four of us stumbled outside. The night air was a balm on my sweat-damp skin.

"What she said," Milton added, combing his hands through his shaggy dark hair. "Why have you been holding out on us?"

I grinned. "I guess I should sing mad more often."

And then, suddenly, Will was there. "Do you mind if I borrow Claire for a minute?"

Without waiting for an answer he grabbed my arm and pulled me around to the side of the house. There wasn't anyone else there, and the only light came from the windows above us. We could hear the rowdy crowd inside but it was about a hundred times quieter than it had been five minutes ago.

"What are you—" I started to say, but then Will was pulling a shirt over my head. He tugged my arms through the sleeves like I was a little kid and stood there glaring at me.

He was bare-chested. He was standing there in jeans and nothing else, which must mean—

I looked down at myself. Will had given me the shirt off his back, which in this case was a football jersey way too big for me.

I started to take it off. "What's your fucking problem? I don't—"

He grabbed my hands and held them away from the hem of the jersey. "I couldn't find your shirt, so you can wear mine instead. This is a football crowd, right? They'll love it."

Will's bare chest was all hard muscle and smooth skin. Remembering the girls who'd been all over him, I felt anger rocketing up from my belly.

"And I guess your little groupies will love this, huh?" I asked, jerking my hands free of Will's grip and gesturing at his bare torso. His jeans hung low on his hips, showing the waistband of his navy blue boxers.

He frowned. "What's that supposed to mean?"

"I mean the girls who looked ready to do you on the couch. What would your girlfriend say if she knew about that?"

His jaw tightened. "Considering she broke up with me two months ago, I'm thinking she wouldn't care a whole hell of a lot."

A hundred things happened inside of me. In the midst of it all, I hung onto being mad.

"I see. So that's your excuse for turning into a manwhore? Your girlfriend broke up with you?"

He looked incredulous. "Are you kidding? I wasn't the one doing a strip tease in front of a hundred strangers. What the hell were you thinking? You're too talented to do that shit. You were belittling yourself."

"I was expressing myself." I reached for the hem of the jersey again. "And I'm going to keep on expressing myself. Maybe I'll lose the bra for the second set. Maybe I'll—"

Will grabbed my hands and we started to struggle, me trying to pull the shirt off and him trying to stop me.

We were both breathing hard. "You're going to rip it," I said through clenched teeth. "Let *go*."

"Only if you promise to—"

"What the hell is going on here?"

I froze. Then I turned around, slowly, and saw Ted standing a few yards away.

In that moment I realized a couple of things. One, I was drunker than I'd realized—drunk enough that I wasn't quite steady on my feet. And two, that little scuffle between me and Will was probably easy to misconstrue.

"What are you doing here?" I asked blankly.

"I saw a clip on YouTube of you singing in your bra, so I thought I'd better get down here." Ted's eyes shifted to Will. "You and I haven't had the pleasure. I'm Claire's boyfriend. Who the fuck are you?"

"He's no one," I said quickly. Will jerked his head around to look at me, and I knew I'd hurt his feelings.

One problem at a time. Ted's your boyfriend; he has to be your priority.

"I'm glad you're here," I said, keeping my focus on Ted. "You'll be able to see our second set."

"Not until you tell me the deal with your first set." Ted looked at Will again. "Would you mind giving us some privacy? You could use the opportunity to put a shirt on."

I'd known Will for a year, and he was always pretty easygoing. Ted was acting a little obnoxious but I didn't think Will would be bothered by it. I expected him to roll his eyes, mutter something under his breath, and take off.

But that wasn't what happened.

Will took three steps forward and stopped right in front of Ted. He had about four inches and fifty pounds on him, and I didn't blame Ted for taking a step back.

"I'd be happy to put on my shirt, but your girlfriend's wearing it at the moment. Maybe if you'd been here to look out for her she wouldn't have to."

"I don't need anyone to look out for me," I sputtered indignantly—but I might as well have been talking to myself.

"That's your shirt?" Ted asked, glancing at the jersey with the big number 12 on it.

"Yeah, that's my shirt. I'm the quarterback of the Hart Panthers."

I'd never heard Will talk like that—like he was bragging about football. If anything, he usually played it down.

"Well, aren't you special. Looking for an excuse to show Claire how tough you are?"

"Not really. But I am looking for an excuse to punch you in the mouth for making her cry."

"I'm not crying," I protested before Ted could say anything. "I haven't *been* crying."

Will turned his scowl on me. "Not tonight. Last year. All those times you came to dinner with red eyes? I knew your so-called boyfriend was to blame."

He was right, although I had no idea how he knew that. I never cried in front of anyone and I never talked about my arguments with Ted.

Ted was staring at me. And then, somehow, the fight changed.

It wasn't a fight anymore. It was a breakup.

I don't know how I knew that, but I did. I could see it in Ted's eyes—a kind of defeated resignation.

But maybe I could still stop it.

I turned to Will almost savagely. "Get out of here."

"I don't—"

"Please, Will. Please."

He looked from me to Ted, who wasn't saying anything. Maybe he saw the same thing in Ted's eyes that I did. Whatever the reason, Will walked off without another word, going around the corner of the house to the front yard and out of sight.

"Don't do this," I said at the same time Ted said, "Claire."

We were both quiet for a second. Then:

"You know when I showed up tonight, and you were arguing with that guy?"

My hands were clenched into fists. Inside me, it felt like my heart was clenched, too.

"There's nothing going on between me and Will."

Ted sighed. "I know. That's not what I—"

"I would never cheat on you."

"I know that, too. Would you please just let me get through this?"

I couldn't let him get through it. I couldn't let him start. But when I opened my mouth to say something, anything, the ache in my throat made it impossible to speak.

And so Ted did.

"The reason I got so upset when I saw you with him . . . it wasn't that I thought you were cheating on me. It was seeing you so alive. So fierce. You and I haven't been like that in a long time."

I didn't say anything. Ted looked at me for a second, and then he took off his glasses, cleaned them with the hem of his shirt, and put them on again.

"The truth is, I don't know if we were ever like that. Tell me the truth, Claire. Do you feel passionate when you're with me?"

I stared at him. "What are you talking about?"

"We're together because it's familiar. Because it feels safe. But not because we're in love."

"That's not true," I said, my voice shaking. "You know I love you."

"Sure. And I love you. But I'm not *in* love with you."

His words were like a knife to my heart. Like he was standing there killing me, only I didn't actually die.

"Ted—"

"It's okay," he said. "You'll be okay. Because you're not in love with me, either."

"How can you—"

"Claire?" It was Jocelyn, popping her head around the corner of the house. "Are you ready to go on? It's time for our second set."

I couldn't speak. I couldn't say a word.

Jocelyn took a step toward us. "Claire?" She looked from me to Ted, the look on her face saying, *I'll kick your ass if you're hurting her.*

Ted shook his head. "Don't worry. I'm leaving."

"Ted!"

He took a step closer to me, but he was already gone. I could see it in his eyes.

"You'll be fine, Claire. You just got used to me, that's all . . . and you're the most loyal person I've ever met. But it's been over between us for a while."

And then he really was gone. I tried to follow, but my feet felt heavy, like they'd been stuck in cement.

Jocelyn came over and grabbed my hand. "Shit. Was that a breakup? Did you guys just break up?"

I didn't want to answer. I didn't want to admit it. Maybe if I nodded instead of saying yes I could still keep it from being true, somehow.

So I nodded. But as soon as I did, I knew it was too late. Ted was gone.

"We can cancel the rest of the gig," Jocelyn was saying. "It won't be a problem. I'll tell them . . ."

"No."

The word came from some place deep inside me—deeper even than the pain of breaking up with my boyfriend.

"Are you sure?" Jocelyn asked.

"Yes. The show will fucking go on."

"But you're crying."

I was?

I put a hand to my face and felt wetness. Jocelyn was right; I was crying.

I used the hem of Will's jersey to wipe the tears away. Then I pulled it off.

"I can't wear this. People will think I'm screwing the quarterback."

"Milton or Burns can lend you theirs."

I nodded. My hat had fallen off during my fight with Will, and now I picked it up from the ground and put it on again.

"Okay," I said. "Let's do this."

CHAPTER THREE

Watching Claire perform was always incredible.

Most people work really hard to protect themselves. To hide who they really are.

But Claire wasn't like that. When she was onstage, she was totally herself. Raw. Naked. She put herself out there so completely it was like you could see into her heart.

The first set had been about anger, needing to feel strong and burn off steam. The second set, after Ted showed up, was about heartache and confusion, guilt and pain—all the emotions you feel after a breakup.

Her voice was like . . . man, I don't even know how to describe it. Pure and sweet and soulful, with the kind of range that could hit the high note in the Star Spangled Banner with no trouble at all. It went through me, somehow, like a blade of fire.

Hearing Claire sing made me burn. Seeing her made me burn.

And now she was single.

"No."

I jerked my head around and saw Andre next to me. After the scene outside I'd gone upstairs to put on a shirt, and by the time I'd come back down the band was playing again. Afraid of what Claire might see in my face if I got too close to her, I was hanging in the back of the room.

"What do you mean, no?"

Between all the beer I'd drunk and the effect Claire had on me I was pretty well buzzed, so I was leaning against the wall. Andre was leaning back, too, his hands in his pockets and his eyes on the band.

He turned his head to look at me. "I mean don't do it. Do not under any circumstances go after Claire tonight."

I could have denied that's what I wanted, or made a joke, or brushed him off. Instead I asked, "Why not? She just broke up with her boyfriend. She's single."

"Because this is a lose-lose situation. If you guys hook up, you're her rebound. If you don't, you'll end up talking all night and comforting her and then you'll be in the friendzone forever."

I tried to think clearly through my buzz. "But what if she needs someone to comfort her?"

"She has people for that. Her band and a dorm full of friends. C'mon, man. Wouldn't she be better off with someone who doesn't want to get into her pants?"

"I don't want to get into her pants. I mean, I do, but not just that. I want more than that. I want—"

"I know, I know. But whatever it is you want, it's not what Claire needs right now. And it's not what you need, either. Just trust me on this and play it cool tonight. Okay?"

Buzzed as I was, I knew Andre was probably right. I didn't want a one-night stand or a permanent spot in the friendzone. If I was serious about getting with Claire, the smart move was to hold off, at least for now.

"Okay."

Andre clapped me on the shoulder, almost knocking me off my feet. "Good man."

He stayed there for one more song and then he took off. I stayed where I was for the rest of the set, resisting the urge to drink any more. I figured the more sober I was, the easier it would be to stay away from Claire.

The set ended and the crowd cheered loud and long, which made me happy.

Claire put down her mic and turned to say something to the band. Now that the show was over, the energy that had kept her going seemed to seep out of her. Her shoulders sagged, and when she turned around again she looked tired and sad.

I took a step toward her before I even realized what I was doing.

A voice in my head was shouting, *She's hurting! Go talk to her!*

But then another voice—a voice that sounded a lot like Andre's—said, *Danger, Will McKenna.*

So I did an about-face, weaving my way through the happy, drunken crowd as I headed for the stairs.

"Will! Hold up, Will!"

I stopped. Then I turned and spotted Claire coming toward me with my jersey in her hand.

It would be rude to walk away now. And anyway, this wasn't my fault. Claire was the one who'd initiated contact. I'd been sticking to the plan, minding my own business, heading for the stairs.

By the time I got that far in my internal monologue, Claire had reached me.

"Hey," she said.

She was sweaty and exhausted and I'd never seen her look more beautiful. The white T-shirt she'd put on—I'd used deductive reasoning to conclude it belonged to the guy on drums who'd done the second set shirtless—was soaked with perspiration and sticking to her stomach. She'd taken off her fedora and her silky blond hair was tucked behind her ears.

I wanted to slide my hands into that hair. I wanted to kiss her. I wanted to haul her into my arms and carry her up to my bedroom.

"Here."

She was holding out my jersey. I took the shirt from her, but before I could say anything she was talking again.

"I'm sorry about before. I mean . . ." She trailed off, frowning down at the floor.

"I'm the one who's sorry, Claire."

She looked up again. "How about we forget it ever happened?"

"Done."

After that we just stood there for a moment, and I was thinking that this was my second chance. I could say good night and head upstairs and—

"The only reason I didn't wear your jersey is that I didn't want everyone to think . . ." She trailed off again.

"No, I get it. It's fine."

I was wishing she had worn it, though. Because then I'd have something that smelled like her.

Say good night and go upstairs.

"So," she said. "Can I ask you a favor?"

Okay, I couldn't say good night and go upstairs just yet.

"Of course."

"Would you mind if I crash here tonight?"

Three words echoed in my head like stones dropping into water.

Crash.

Here.

Tonight.

"Um . . ."

I was wishing like hell I wasn't so buzzed. How was I supposed to navigate this?

"The band is going out to celebrate but I'm not really up for that. I'd go back to the dorm but Ted is staying in my room and I'm not sure when he's leaving. I'd rather not—" Her face twisted in sudden pain, and in that moment I would have walked through fire to make her feel better.

"Of course. No problem." My mind struggled to function. "You can stay in my room and I'll stay—" Where the hell was I going to stay? "—somewhere."

Would this relegate me to the friendzone forever? No, I decided. Not if I got her settled in my room and left quick.

No talking late into the night, no commiserating over ice cream, no braiding each others' hair. Just good night and sweet dreams and close the door.

Claire looked relieved. "Thank you, Will. I mean it. Thank you."

I'd never seen eyes as blue as hers. Sometimes blue eyes can look kind of washed out, but not Claire's. They were as deep and wide and rich as the sky.

"Would you mind if I go up now?" she asked. "Then you can keep on partying or whatever."

I'd never felt less like partying, but that would be one excuse to get me out of the room once Claire was in it.

"Sure. Come on."

It was slow going through the crowd, but it wasn't until we were halfway up the stairs that we faced a real obstacle.

"Where are you two headed?"

It was Andre, coming down as we were going up. He planted himself in the middle of the stairway and folded his arms, making it clear that the path to the second floor went through his large and intimidating person.

Claire blinked up at him, her blue eyes a little unfocused, and I realized for the first time that she'd been drinking, too.

"Wow, you're big. I mean, I always knew you were big, but—" She glanced down. "Oh. You're standing on the step above us. That probably makes you even bigger, right?"

I did my best to appear less drunk than Claire. "Claire's staying here tonight," I said in what I hoped was a responsible-sounding voice. "The band is heading out to party and she's not in the mood. And since her ex might be in her room, she doesn't feel like going back to Bracton. So I offered to let her stay in my room, while I—" Inspiration struck. "While I stay in your room. On the floor. In my sleeping bag."

Andre frowned. "I guess that makes sense."

There, see? I was making sense. "I'm going to get Claire settled and then come back downstairs."

Andre finally stepped aside. "Okay. I'll see you down there."

Claire moved past him and I followed her, climbing the last few stairs to the second floor.

The upstairs hall was crowded with people, all waiting for the bathroom. Claire paused at the end of the line. "I need to—"

I steered her away. "I have my own bathroom."

"You do? But won't people be waiting for that one, too?"

I shook my head. "I locked my room before things got started."

"Wow. So you have a private bathroom? Fancy."

I grinned as we stopped in front of my door. "Yeah, real fancy." I fished my key out of my pocket and let us in, ushering Claire inside and closing the door behind us.

It was suddenly a lot quieter. This was an old house, and the doors and walls were pretty solid. You could still hear people out in the hallway, but the conversations were a soft blur.

Claire was looking around. Standing behind her, I looked around, too—through her eyes.

When we first moved in here, I was all gung-ho. This was my first time living somewhere that wasn't my parents' house or a dorm, and I'd been full of plans to paint my room and put up some framed pictures. But preseason practice started the next day, and once I got caught up in football I never got around to painting . . . or much of anything else.

The walls weren't terrible, but they hadn't been painted for a while and the off-white color had darkened over the years. There were also paler patches where a previous owner had hung pictures. I'd put up a few posters over some of those spots, but since I'd used Scotch tape instead of frames and picture-hanging hardware, I hadn't exactly classed up the joint.

The posters weren't too bad—meaning, they weren't porn stills like the ones Delford had in his room. Not that I can't ogle naked women with the best of them, but I wouldn't put that shit on my walls. I stuck mostly to sports, music, and Deadpool.

There were water stains on the ceiling and on the floor around the radiator. The wood floors themselves weren't bad—a little uneven, maybe—but they were covered with more dirty laundry than I remembered being there.

"It's a little, uh, messy," I said, moving past Claire and kicking some of the clothes out of the way.

"That's okay," Claire said, looking over to her right—where the bed was.

I'd had a decent amount of alcohol that night but nothing epic, and the last drink I'd had was more than an hour ago. Sobriety shivered through me like an electric charge, followed by a different kind of inebriation.

Claire was in my room.

God knew I'd imagined her here a hundred times. But in all those fantasies, she was here for sex. The fantasies usually started with me tearing off her clothes or her tearing off mine, depending on my mood, and ended with the two of us in my bed, our naked bodies tangled together in blissful post-sex slumber.

But tonight wasn't going to end that way. Because Andre was right—if something happened between me and Claire right now, I'd only be her rebound.

We spoke at the same time.

"Okay, so—"

"Ted is really—"

We both stopped. Then I asked: "Ted is really what?"

Claire put her arms around her waist and started to walk, slowly, around my room.

"Neat. Like, OCD neat. It drives me crazy."

This was the other thing Andre had warned me about. Claire obviously wanted to talk about Ted. But if I let myself get sucked into that, wouldn't it be a deep dive into the friendzone?

I backed up and put my hand on the doorknob. "I should go back downstairs," I said. "I'm supposed to be cohosting this thing, right? And you should try to get some sleep."

Claire sat down on the edge of my bed. The mattress barely gave at all, even though it squeaked and groaned every time I sat on it.

"Okay."

That was all she said. But her blue eyes turned bright, and then she blinked hard and looked down at her feet.

It felt like someone reached into my chest and yanked out my heart.

It was one of those deals where time seems to slow, giving you a chance to make an important decision.

For some reason I thought of my mom and stepdad. And once I did that, it was over.

Sometimes it sucks to have the two most decent, unselfish people in the world as your parents.

"Unless you need to talk or something."

She looked up again, and this time the tears leaked out. She used the back of her hand to wipe them away. "That would be great. I mean, if you don't mind. I . . ."

She hugged herself again, and her voice got so soft I could barely hear her. "I just feel so lonely."

My heart squeezed in my chest again. "I don't mind."

She kicked off her sandals and moved up to the head of the bed, leaning back against my pillows and wrapping her arms around her knees. She looked pensive, and I knew I was about to hear a lot more about Ted than I'd ever wanted to.

I went over to my desk, spun the chair around, and sat with my arms folded along the back.

Then I took a deep breath and prepared to be noble.

"So, what happened with you guys tonight?"

CHAPTER FOUR

I woke up slowly and in stages.

The first thing I was aware of was my head. It was a little foggy but not too bad—not my worst hangover by any stretch.

The next thing I was aware of was my body.

But it wasn't just my body. It was my body and Will's.

I was lying on my left side. The big, solid bulk of him was behind me, his arm draped over my waist.

I did a quick check of my memory. No, Will and I hadn't had sex. We hadn't fooled around.

We hadn't even kissed.

He'd been the perfect gentleman and friend. He'd let me ramble on about my stupid failed relationship without once telling me to just shut the hell up, which alone should qualify him for a medal.

So how had we ended up like this? The plan had been for me to crash in his room while he stayed somewhere else.

As the night had gone on I'd gotten sleepier and fuzzier and my rambling more disjointed until finally Will said, "You're wiped out. I'm going to go and let you get some sleep, okay?"

That had been enough to wake me up. If Will left, I knew exactly what I'd do.

I'd call Ted.

"Don't go."

I was ashamed of the words the moment they came out of my mouth. They were pathetic. They were needy. They were—

"I have to go."

I stared at him. His voice was different, suddenly. Rougher.

"I'm sorry," I said, feeling even worse. "I've kept you away from your own party. You're right. You should go. I'll be fine."

He'd been sitting on his desk chair this whole time, listening to me talk. Now he got to his feet and started to pace, his hands stuck in his pockets.

"I'm not worried about the party. I don't give a shit about the party. I just . . ."

I watched him prowl around his own room like an animal in a cage. I was still a little buzzed, not to mention exhausted and sort of hollowed out, but I tried to figure out what Will was thinking.

Suddenly I remembered something I'd forgotten about.

"Oh my God."

Will stopped pacing and stared at me. "What is it? What's wrong?"

"Your girlfriend. You guys broke up, too. Oh my God, I'm so selfish. All my babbling is reminding you of that, isn't it? I'm making you think about it. I'm so sorry. Do you want to talk about it, or do you just want to get back to the party?" I answered my own question. "Of course you want to get back to the party. I'm sorry. You should go."

Will stared at me for another moment. Then his shoulders sort of sagged and he combed a hand through his hair. "Okay."

He sounded almost hopeless, and I felt terrible.

"Unless you want to talk. You listened to me talk forever. Please, Will, stay and talk to me. I've been a shitty friend. I didn't even ask you about her. But I'm asking you now. Talk to me." I realized something. "God, I don't even remember her name. I'm the worst friend in the world. What's her name?"

He looked even more hopeless. "Lissa."

I started to ask something else. But the alcohol I'd drunk and my emotions about Ted and the post-gig exhaustion sort of tangled up inside me, and before I could stop myself, I was crying.

Then Will was there with his arm around my shoulders. He held me as I cried, murmuring something soothing and comforting, while I said *Don't go* over and over.

And that, somehow, had led to us spending the night together. Well, not *together*, but side by side.

Last night it had felt innocent. We were just two friends comforting each other after our breakups.

But this morning, it felt completely different.

A rush of something went through me. No, not a rush. A rush is fast, and this was slow and sweet, like honey.

Even though my head was foggy, my body felt wonderful. Warm and safe and . . .

Alive.

I wanted to stay like this forever. Will's presence seemed to drive away all the miserable emotions of yesterday—the fear and anger and sadness and guilt, and the horrible overwhelming sense of failure and loneliness.

How could I be lonely if Will was with me?

But then, slowly, I thought about what that meant.

I'd broken up with Ted last night. *Last night.*

I wasn't thinking clearly. I wasn't being rational. I was—

And then Will made this sound—a sort of half snore, half snort. Was he waking up?

His arm around me tightened, and every cell in my body responded.

Then I had to stifle a gasp. Behind me, Will pressed himself closer. And there, nestled right against my butt, was either a piece of lead pipe or Will's hard-on.

He was hard. Wanting me.

But in his sleep. Right? That didn't count. Guys woke up with erections all the time. It was biology. Nonspecific biology.

He would have reacted that way no matter who was in bed with him—and probably if he was alone, too. It didn't have anything to do with me.

But maybe I could make it have to do with me.

I could turn around in his arms and wake him up. I could kiss him, say his name, make him say mine.

Claire.

And oh, did I want to. I wanted to hear him say my name with hunger, with longing, with—

Love.

A rush of shame followed the rush of lust. Love? I had loved Ted. We were together for four years. What was wrong with me?

Slowly, I eased myself out from under Will's arm. Slowly, I moved to the edge of the bed. Slowly, I—

"Claire?"

I whipped my head around and saw that Will's eyes were open. His expression was confused and sleepy, but he was definitely awake.

"Good morning," I said, trying to sound cheerful and normal and like everything between us was still exactly the same, even though a moment ago I'd thought about using him to forget about Ted. My voice was a little raspy, but I'd sung my guts out last night.

"You okay?" he asked, and a shiver went through me. His voice was raspy too, but in a different way. Rough and gravelly and so . . .

I got a grip on myself.

"Oh, sure. Of course. I mean, it was a rough night, but I'm fine. Thanks for letting me stay here. Really. I mean it."

"No problem."

He was a little more awake now, and he was close enough to touch. I could sink back into bed and crawl into his arms and we could—

What? Have sex? Decide to be boyfriend and girl-friend? Get married and have kids?

I got up and found my sandals. "Okay, then. I guess I'll head back to Bracton now."

"Are you sure you're okay?" he asked. "You sound kind of . . . I don't know. Weird."

I had my back to him while I slipped on my sandals. Now I turned to face him, figuring it would be safe to look at him now that I was out of bed with my shoes on.

I was wrong.

He was sitting up, which gave me a view of his upper body.

Man, he was perfect. How had I not noticed before? I mean really, really noticed?

Maybe there was something to be said for the whole sports thing. Because every inch of Will was ripped, from the heavy bands of muscle on his arms and shoulders to the powerful chest and flat abs. And I felt weak, almost helpless, in the face of that overwhelming masculinity.

I'm strong, that masculinity seemed to say. *I can take care of you.*

I cringed internally. Was that what I wanted? Some guy to take care of me?

It wasn't just his physical strength that was so appealing. There was also his kindness, the decency that seemed to radiate from him. His green eyes were sweet and full of concern, his face handsome and a little scruffy, his auburn hair tousled and touchable.

He was basically a six-foot-two package of smoking hot male protectiveness, designed to push every emotional—and physical—button in my female self.

Everything in me was screaming *stay.*

"I have to go," I said abruptly.

I kept enough presence of mind to turn once I had my hand on the doorknob.

"Thanks again for last night, Will. Really. You're a good friend."

And then I fled.

* * *

When I got back to Bracton, Ted was gone.

I leaned against the doorjamb, looking around my room and feeling like crap. The only thing I really wanted to do was crawl into my bed and sleep for a hundred years.

Down the hall, I heard another door open. I turned my head and Tamsin was there.

She hadn't bothered to dye her roots for a while, so her hair was a mix of girl-next-door brown and Goth black. The rest of her picked up on the theme. Her sky blue T-shirt and jeans were girl-next-door, but the black eyeliner running down her cheeks was Goth.

It was something else, too.

"Tamsin? What's wrong?"

I forgot my own stupid troubles for a second to focus on my friend, who'd obviously been crying her eyes out.

"Oscar and I broke up last night."

"Oh no. I'm so sorry." I rushed over and gave her a hug. "Ted and I broke up last night, too. There must be something really sucky in the air."

Tamsin hugged me back. "I guess so."

A minute later we were in her room, her on her bed and me on Rikki's.

"Oscar isn't coming back to Hart this year. He's going to travel instead." Tamsin grabbed a tissue from the box beside her bed and swabbed at the black mess under her eyes, and I didn't have the heart to tell her she was making it worse. "I offered to go with him. To take the year off and follow him around South America like some kind of puppy dog. Pathetic, right? But he said no, this is his hero's journey and he has to go alone."

I stared at her. "His *hero's journey?* My God, that's the most egotistical thing I've ever heard. Seriously, Tamsin—I know you feel like shit right now, but I'm thinking you dodged a bullet here."

She blew her nose into the eyeliner-stained tissue. "You do?"

"Are you kidding me? His hero's journey? Take a second to contemplate the sheer unadulterated bullshit of that."

She looked down at the crumpled tissue in her hand. After a moment the corners of her mouth quirked up, and then she was laughing.

I laughed, too. I laughed until my stomach muscles hurt, and it felt great.

It was a catharsis.

Maybe that's what I'd wanted from Will this morning, when I'd fought the urge to crawl into bed with him and have rebound sex. A catharsis.

But you can't use people like that. You can't use one guy to purge another guy from your system.

I got up from Rikki's bed and went over to Tamsin's, sitting cross-legged beside her.

"I have an idea."

Tamsin stopped laughing. "You sound serious."

"I am. I'm totally serious." I grabbed her hands. "I think we should make a solemn vow."

"A solemn vow? Dude, I haven't even had breakfast yet."

"No, listen. Listen." I took a deep breath. "I think we should swear off men."

Tamsin looked horrified. "Are you nuts? A breakup is no reason to swear off men. That's a massive overcorrection."

"Just give me a minute to make my case, okay? I swear I'm onto something here."

"How about we go down to the dining hall and you tell me over breakfast?"

I was suddenly starving. "Okay. Deal."

A little while later our trays were full of eggs and pancakes and bacon and we were sitting at one of the small tables along the wall.

"All right, lay it on me," Tamsin said, stirring sugar into her coffee.

I finished a bite of toast and leaned forward. "This isn't an anti-man thing. This is a pro-us thing. Here's my question. What would our lives be like if we didn't pour so much energy into guys? Emotional energy, sexual energy, whatever? What if we put all that energy into ourselves? Our classes? Our creativity? Our friendships?"

Tamsin took a gulp of coffee and set her cup down. "You know, I did read an article about tantric celibacy over the summer. I thought it was bullshit at the time but it's kind of been percolating in my mind."

"Tantric celibacy? What's that?"

Tamsin poured maple syrup on her pancakes. "What you were saying. Taking sexual energy and turning it inward. Recycling it. Apparently it can unleash all sorts of inner power."

I slapped my palm on the table. "That's what I'm talking about! Let's do it."

"It sounds good right now, sure. But I don't want to say *yes, let's do it* and then give up in a week when I meet a hot guy at a party. Because, to be completely honest, I really like sex. I'm not sure I can go without it."

"I didn't say it would be easy. But it's worth a try. How about a semester? What if we commit to celibacy and singlehood for one semester? We can last that long. I know we can." I paused. "And it's not just sex. I mean, it's not just about keeping men out of our bodies. It's about keeping them out of our heads, too. And our hearts. And seeing what we can do when all that mental and sexual and emotional energy is freed up."

Tamsin shook her head slowly. "Damn, you're inspiring when you get going. You really think we can do this?"

"Absolutely. I know we can. Especially if we have each other to lean on. And we should let Rikki and Dyshell and everyone know what we're doing. They'll support us. If we feel like we're weakening or something, we'll have people to call or text or whatever. We can do this, Tamsin."

I went on. "And it doesn't mean that guys can't be in our lives. Just the opposite. Guy friends are okay. Maybe our relationships with guys can be even deeper and better like this. Don't you think sex warps our perspective sometimes? I mean, even when I was with Ted, I sort of filtered guys through this sexual lens. Were they attracted to me? Would I be attracted to them if I wasn't with Ted?"

An image of Will from that morning flashed into my mind. "And I'd wonder what it would it be like with them. You know? And I'd kind of hope they were into me even though I wasn't available. Like the more guys that want me, the more worthwhile I am. Which is *fucked up*."

I pushed my tray to the side and leaned forward, resting my forearms on the table and clasping my hands together. "We're not worthwhile because we can attract guys, and we're not worthless if we can't."

"Of course not." Tamsin finished her coffee in one long swallow. "And I'm not powerful just because I'm good in bed. That's not the best thing about me."

"And our male friends deserve better from us. We should be able to focus on real friendship stuff with them, too."

"It is hard to do that sometimes," Tamsin admitted. "I mean, the sex thing always seems to be there under the surface. Waiting to bubble up."

"I know. But we don't have to let that be more important than everything else."

Tamsin nodded. "Okay, I'm in. This semester, sex and romance aren't on the menu."

"We'll focus on classes. Family. Friends. Music for me and theater for you."

"Yes. Except not family for me, because I hate them. But all the other stuff is cool."

I sat back in my chair. "Man, I feel empowered. Do you feel empowered?"

"So empowered."

I held up a piece of bacon. "To the Semester of Us."

Tamsin grabbed a piece of her own bacon and tapped it against mine. "The Semester of Us."

CHAPTER FIVE

I had strength training and practice that day, but Claire was all I could think about.

I could still feel her in my arms. Her warmth and sweetness pressed against me . . . the rush of heat and hunger that made me harder than I'd ever been in my life.

She'd taken off pretty fast that morning, which I understood. I was even glad, because Andre was right. I didn't want to be Claire's rebound. I didn't want to be the next guy she was with.

I wanted to be the last guy she was with.

The problem was, I had no clue how to make that happen. Claire had just broken up with her boyfriend. How did I avoid being a rebound or landing in the friendzone?

If the answer was not to see her for a while, then I was screwed. Because the only thing I wanted to do after practice was see Claire.

After I showered and changed I went to the dining hall at Bracton for dinner. Claire wasn't down yet, but it was still early. I headed up to her room and knocked on the door.

"Come in!"

Claire was sitting on the floor with her back against the bed, her guitar in her lap. She was wearing jeans and a Hart University T-shirt. Her feet were bare, and I noticed that her toenails were painted pink.

If there was any doubt I was crazy about this girl it was now completely wiped away. After spending the night with her in my arms, even platonically, all I wanted to do was hold her again.

I was like a magnet that only worked around Claire.

"Hey," I said, forcing myself to keep my distance.

She scrambled to her feet and put the guitar on her bed. "What's up? What are you doing here?"

She sounded a little cautious. Was she nervous I might make a move? If so, it was a good thing I'd come prepared with a reason for stopping by.

Her top from last night wasn't much more than a scrap of material, and I'd been able to stuff it in my back pocket. Now I pulled it out.

"I found your shirt this morning," I said.

She looked relieved, which wasn't great for my ego. Was she that happy I wasn't coming onto her?

"Wow, I forgot I left it there. Thanks, Will."

"Sure."

I walked over and held it out. Our hands brushed when she took it, and a jolt of electricity shot through me.

Did she feel it, too?

She frowned and took a step back.

Her eyes were on the shirt, which she was sort of squeezing in her hands. I had a chance to stare at her without her knowing.

I'd never seen eyes that blue or lips that soft. I'd never known a girl with skin like Claire's, skin that makes your palms itch and your whole body ache.

"Are you going down to dinner?" I asked.

"Yes," she said, tossing the top onto her bed. "Have you eaten yet? Do you want to go down with me?"

"Yeah, that sounds good."

"All right, let's go." She hesitated. "I'm glad you're here, actually. I have a kind of announcement I want to make to everybody."

Up until that point, I'd been feeling pretty good. Just seeing Claire made it seem like everything was going to be okay, somehow.

But now I felt a chill.

What was she planning to announce? That she and Ted were getting back together? That she was dropping out of Hart? What?

The thought of being here without Claire was painful. More than painful. I tried not to worry about it as we went downstairs to the dining hall, but I had to squeeze my hands into fists to keep from tossing Claire over my shoulder and carrying her off to my cave.

I had to wait another ten minutes before I could find out what was up. The line for food was long, and then, once we were finally sitting down, Claire wanted to wait until everyone she was expecting was there.

In the end it was Dyshell, Tamsin, Rikki, Sam, Julia, Mena, and Izzy. Most of the people I knew from Bracton.

I knew some better than others. Mena was from London and planning to be a doctor, like Claire. Julia was the quietest one of the group, a redhead who was studying dance.

Sam was the only other guy at the table. I liked him in spite of the fact that he preferred basketball to football, and when he and Rikki had hooked up last year it was a huge relief to everyone. I mean, unspoken love is romantic and all, but the way those two had fought their feelings during the whole first semester was enough to make you shoot yourself.

When they'd finally gotten together, they'd done it with a vengeance. They were the most sickening couple on campus. Watching them now, it was obvious they were still totally and completely in love.

Rikki's roommate Tamsin was there, but not Tamsin's boyfriend Oscar. I was worried that Claire would insist on waiting for him, too, but once Izzy joined us Claire tapped on her glass like someone about to give a toast.

"Okay, you guys, here we go. Tamsin and I have made a decision." She paused for emphasis. "We're going cold turkey on relationships this semester. That includes hookups, one-night stands, love, romance, and everything in between. And we're asking for your help. You can't fix us up with anyone, even if you think they'd be perfect for us. And if we call you or text you to say we're in danger—like, we've been drinking and there's a cute guy and we're about to succumb—you have to help us resist temptation."

There was a moment of silence around the table. The first one to break it was Dyshell.

"Of course we'll support you if you want to be single for a while. But—"

Tamsin raised an eyebrow. "There's a but?"

"*But* you're both dealing with breakups right now. Don't you think you might be reacting to that?"

Tamsin shook her head. "That's part of it, sure. But it's not the biggest part." She waved a hand at Rikki and Sam. "These two are one thing. I mean, they're perfect for each other. But they're also independent, you know? Rikki was single for a long time before she finally got with Sam. I know Rikki's fine on her own because I've seen her on her own. Sam, too." She gestured at Julia. "You're single, and you're doing great. You're focused on your classes and dance and all that." She looked at Mena. "You're pansexual or whatever, and you're doing great too. You don't do jealousy or dependence or anything like that. And Izzy, you're in a long-distance thing with a guy from back home, right? And it doesn't even faze you. Me, I used to get separation anxiety when Oscar went to the bathroom. That's not healthy."

Claire nodded her agreement. "I'm the same way. I was so wrapped up in Ted, you know? We started dating when I was a sophomore in high school. We just had our four year anniversary. That's, like, twenty percent of my life. And when he broke up with me, it was like the world had ended. Like I was empty inside." She took a breath. "I don't want to feel empty just because I'm not with a guy." Her eyes met mine for an instant, and then she looked away. "And I don't want to fill that emptiness with someone else just because I'm afraid to be alone. I don't want to use anyone like that. And . . .

and I want to find out who I am when it's just me. You know?"

"Of course," Rikki said quickly. "I totally get what you mean. And we'll be here for whatever you guys need." She glanced around the table like a scout leader. "Right?"

Nods of agreement from all of us. "Right."

Claire looked relieved. "Thanks, everybody." She raised her soda glass. "Here's to flying solo!"

The rest of us raised our glasses. "To flying solo."

I was pretty quiet during dinner, but I didn't think anyone noticed. Then, when I got up to leave, Claire got up too.

"Are you going back to your place?" she asked.

"Yeah."

"Can I walk out with you?"

"Sure."

It was twilight, and the air was cooler than it had been yesterday. We stood on the dorm steps for a moment, enjoying the breeze, and then Claire bumped my arm with her shoulder.

"Could I talk to you for a sec? Before you go?"

"Sure," I said again, wondering what was coming.

She sat down on the top step, tucking one foot underneath her. "I just wanted to thank you again for last night. I hope staying over like that didn't send any mixed signals. You know, in light of, uh—"

I sat down too. "Your celibacy pledge?"

That made her smile. "Yes."

I stuck my hands in my pockets, staring up at the sky. It was only eight o'clock but the moon was already visible. It was a little more than half full—a gibbous moon, I remembered Sam telling us last year.

"No mixed signals," I said now.

"Okay. Good." A short pause. "Friends?"

I turned and looked at her again. The truth was, I didn't want to be friends with Claire Stone. But if that was my only option?

It was better than nothing.

"Friends," I agreed.

A smile spread over her face, and I decided it was a lot better than nothing.

"Awesome. Because I want to go to your game next weekend."

Next Saturday was the first game of the season. "Seriously? You hate football."

"I don't hate football exactly. I'm just not a fan. But part of my whole no-romance thing is wanting to be a better friend. When you're all wrapped up in a relationship, you're not the kind of friend you should be." Her smile faded a little. "Or maybe that's just me. I mean, Rikki's still an awesome friend even though she's with Sam. But I didn't go to a single game of yours last year."

Considering I rode the bench all season, that was okay with me.

Thinking about Claire at our season opener filled my head with stupid fantasies. Maybe if I played the game of my life, I could make Claire swoon with my awesome skills and heroic quarterbacking.

Or, I could fuck up and throw six interceptions.

But you don't win football games by worrying about them.

"My mom and stepdad are coming out," I said. "They're getting two of my four tickets. Do you want the other pair? You could bring Tamsin."

Claire smiled. "I think Tamsin knows less about football than I do. I'll ask her, though—or maybe Rikki. Dyshell's probably got a ticket from Andre, right?"

"Yeah." I was quiet for a moment. "I'm really glad you're going. And you should hang out with us after the game."

"Who's 'us'?"

"Some of the guys on the team. We'll be at the house. Come by whenever you want."

She wrinkled her nose. "A party like last night?"

"No, not like that. It'll be a lot smaller. No band, no keg. I mean, there'll be drinking, but it won't be crazy."

A lock of her blond hair fell forward and she tucked it behind her ear. "That sounds fun. I'll be there."

"Flying solo, right?"

She punched me on the shoulder. "Are you making fun of me?"

"No way," I said with injured innocence. "I'd never make fun of you." I paused. "Seriously, I think it's great that you want to focus on yourself for a while. Your music and your classes and all that."

And then something happened. As I spoke those words, I realized I actually meant them.

I did think it was great. Claire was an awesome person, and she deserved a chance to realize it. Maybe if she spent some time focusing on herself, she'd see what I saw.

Her beauty. Her strength. Her talent.

And if being her friend would help her see all that, then that's what I'd be.

Her friend.

CHAPTER SIX

After Will left that night I felt depressed. I couldn't figure out why until later, when I was in bed trying to fall asleep.

My pledge was less than twelve hours old and my mind was filled with thoughts of a guy.

Thoughts of Will.

I replayed those moments yesterday morning over and over. The way it felt to be in bed with him. How safe, how warm, how . . .

How sexy.

And that's why I'd felt depressed after he left tonight. Because even though I was serious about my pledge to be single, a part of me had been wishing that Will would try to talk me out of it. That he was attracted to me like I was attracted to him. That he wanted me so much he would try to convince me to abandon the pledge and be with him.

That's how pathetic I was. And that's why I'd made the pledge in the first place. I didn't want to see guys as potential boyfriends first and friends second, and I didn't want to see myself as a girlfriend-in-waiting.

I wanted to be a person.

I knew I was making the right decision, and I was glad that Will was supporting me.

But it still took me a while to fall asleep.

* * *

"I can't believe you dragged me to a football game," Rikki said, squinting in the bright sunlight.

"I didn't *drag* you. I asked if you wanted to go and you said yes."

"It seemed like a good idea at the time. But I feel out of place."

I looked around at the other fans in the stadium, most of them wearing the navy blue and white of the Hart Panthers. I was wearing a short-sleeved pink sweater and Rikki was wearing a black T-shirt, and neither one of us had our faces painted or was holding up blue and white pompoms or foam fingers or any other visible signs of fandom.

"It's like some kind of weird cult," Rikki muttered.

I sort of agreed with her, but I felt compelled to defend the experience. "Will says it's no different from music fans wearing band T-shirts when they go to a concert."

Rikki nudged me with her elbow and pointed out a row of male students not far away. Eight of them were standing up, shirtless, and they each had a letter painted in navy blue on their bare chests.

P-A-N-T-H-E-R-S

"Okay, maybe it's a little different," I conceded. "I wonder if they do that in November."

Then I noticed a couple in their forties making their way toward us. The man was big and blond and the woman was beautiful—Debra Messing beautiful—with long red hair and a Panthers T-shirt.

I grabbed Rikki's arm. "Those are Will's folks. His mom and his stepdad."

Rikki looked at me curiously. "Well, you knew they were coming, didn't you? Why are you freaking out?"

Was I freaking out?

"I'm not freaking out," I said, letting go of Rikki's arm.

But I was. And when I looked into my heart, it wasn't hard to see why.

I wanted them to like me. I wanted Will's mom and stepdad to think I was great. I wanted them to tell their son that he ought to be dating a girl like me. That I was way better than Lissa.

A quick pulse of shame brought me up short. What was wrong with me?

"Excuse us," Will's mother said, smiling as she and her husband edged past Rikki and me on their way to their seats. I waited until they were sitting before I said,

"Um, hi. Are you Mr. and Mrs. McKenna?"

Will's mom had taken the seat next to me and now she turned with a big smile on her face.

"Yes, but please call me Holly. Are you friends of Will's?"

I couldn't stop staring at her. Up close like this I could see the resemblance. She and her son had the same gorgeous green eyes.

"Is something wrong?" she asked after a moment, and I realized I needed to say something. *Yes, we're friends of his.*

"You're so pretty," was what I came out with.

Instead of looking at me like I was crazy, Will's mom started to laugh. "Wow, that's a nice thing to hear in a stadium full of college students. Honey, did you hear that?"

Her husband was completely absorbed in the action on the field—football players in their helmets and uniforms doing stretches and calisthenics. Holly elbowed him in the ribs and he turned impatiently.

"What?"

She nodded toward me and Rikki. "These are friends of Will's."

Alex's expression turned contrite immediately. "I'm sorry. I'm always useless on game day, as my wife will tell you. It's great to meet you," he went on, reaching out across Holly to hold out a hand. "My name's Alex."

"I'm Claire," I said as I shook his hand. The selfish wench part of me looked closely to see if there was a flash of recognition on either one of their faces—a sign that Will had mentioned me to them.

Nope.

"And this is Rikki," I went on.

"Nice to meet you," she said. "You're from Ohio, right? Did you drive out for the game?"

Alex's attention was back on the field, and it was Holly who answered. "No, we flew in. We won't be able to be here for every game but we couldn't miss this one. It's Will's first start at QB. In college, anyway."

She said that like we must know it, too. And maybe Will had mentioned it at some point. But if so, I hadn't thought the fact was important enough to actually remember and take note of.

My selfishness apparently had more than one layer.

I decided I wouldn't pretend to know more than I did. "I didn't realize Will wasn't a starter last year. The truth is, I've never been to a game before. I don't know much about football."

"Me, either," Rikki put in. "We're total neophytes. I hope you're not embarrassed to be sitting near us."

Holly grinned. "Oh, no. Believe me, I've been there. I used to hate football, even when my own son started playing. But eventually I got interested. It's actually pretty fun when you get into it. Would you like me to explain things to you?"

"That would be great."

"All right." She pointed toward the Panthers players. "That's Will, of course—number 12."

I hadn't actually spotted him before. The players all looked the same to me in their uniforms and helmets, and I'd forgotten about the numbers on their jerseys.

I looked where Holly was pointing and my heart skipped a beat.

I'd never seen Will in uniform before. The pads and everything made him look big and powerful, and the way his pants hugged his butt . . .

I shouldn't be thinking about his butt. Not with his mother sitting right next to me.

"See those three players lining up across the field? Those are his receivers. They're about to run some practice routes."

I called up my sketchy knowledge of the game. "The receivers catch the passes, right?"

"Right."

Just then Will cocked his arm back and threw. Seeing the perfect arc of the ball, its tight spiraling motion in the air, and the way it landed with flawless precision in the arms of the player catching it, I felt a tingle run through all my nerve endings.

I'd never thought there could be any poetry to football. But maybe I was wrong.

"That was good, wasn't it?" I asked.

Holly laughed. "Yes, that was good."

"Damn good," Alex put in. "He looks sharp today."

"My husband was his high school coach, so he likes to take credit for Will's arm."

"Not his strength," Alex said with a grin. "Just his accuracy."

I started to ask another question, but just then the players jogged off the field and the band started to play.

"We'll be kicking off soon," Holly said.

She sat up a little straighter and I saw energy sparking from her very pores. All around us, I could feel the same kind of energy coming from the fans. They started a chant I couldn't understand until they got to the *Panthers, Panthers, Panthers!* part.

It reminded me of something. Then, as the announcer started calling out the names of the players and they came out of the tunnel on the other side of the field, I realized what it was.

The fans all surged to their feet and Rikki and I surged with them. It was impossible not to.

Just like at a rock concert.

Okay, so maybe Will had a point.

* * *

It turns out that football is exciting. Thrilling. Even terrifying sometimes, like when a bunch of really, really big guys in bright red jerseys swarm toward a friend of yours.

Every time it happened my heart leapt into my mouth. A few times Will just barely got the ball away, either in a handoff to a running back or in a pass, before being knocked to the ground. He was sacked twice, the second time so brutally that I grabbed Holly's arm before I realized what I was doing.

"Oh my God, I'm so sorry," I said, snatching my hand away.

Holly shook her head. "Don't worry about it. I know exactly how you feel." She put her arm around my shoulders and squeezed.

On the field, Andre grabbed Will's hand and hauled him to his feet.

"There, see?" Holly said. "He's getting up. He's fine."

Another thing that made the game tense—and gripping—was how close it was. The first half ended with the Panthers down by three. We came out in the second half and scored a touchdown, and it was looking like we might win by four when the other team scored in the fourth quarter.

We were down by three again with a minute left in the game.

"They'll play for a tie and overtime," Alex said. "All Will has to do is get them into field goal range. They've got a good kicker."

And for a few plays it looked like that would happen. A short gain, a short gain, a first down—and then, disaster. Will was sacked for a big loss with sixteen seconds left to play.

The crowd groaned with one voice. Out of time-outs, Will hurried his players back to the line and called one more play—all he'd have time for before the end of the game.

He backpedaled with the ball, which meant a pass was coming. At the same time, a sea of red jerseys came toward him looking like the apocalypse about to happen.

Will stayed calm. He slipped out of one tackle, evaded another, and then planted his back foot and threw the ball.

And I mean he threw that sucker. It sailed over the field like it had wings, and down near the goal line I saw one lone receiver who'd managed, somehow, to get all the way down there—probably because he was running like a bat out of hell. But was he going fast enough to get under the ball?

At the five yard line he turned his head, made a perfect catch, and crossed into the end zone.

All around us the fans erupted into shouts and cheers, dancing in the stands like a bunch of lunatics—

and Rikki and I were doing the exact same thing. We were jumping up and down and screaming, and then we were hugging Holly and Alex like we'd known them for years.

I couldn't remember the last time I'd felt so purely happy. Call it mob psychology if you want, but I left the stadium flying high, cheering for those crazy shirtless guys with their navy blue body paint and doing high fives with total strangers.

Rikki had plans with Sam, so I dropped her off at Bracton before heading to Will's house. I thought about going upstairs to shower and change first, but I didn't. For one thing, I didn't think that was something a friend would do, and I was determined to be Will's friend. For another, I was too excited to see him to wait. I drove to his place, parked, and went inside.

Except for a guy and a girl I didn't know, I was the first one there.

Okay, so maybe I could have spared the time for a shower.

The guy and the girl were making out on the couch. I wandered into the kitchen to be out of their way, but I could still hear them panting and moaning.

After a minute of that I went upstairs to Will's room. I didn't think he'd mind if I waited there for him.

My focus was different now from the last time I was here. I wasn't drunk, for one thing, and I hadn't just broken up with my boyfriend.

I was walking around slowly, looking at his books and posters, when the door opened behind me. I spun around and there was Will, standing in the doorway looking surprised.

"Hey!" I took a step forward and started talking. "I'm so sorry, I hope it's okay for me to be here. There was a couple downstairs really going at it and I felt sort of uncomfortable, so . . ."

"It's no problem. You can come up here anytime."

I relaxed, and then I noticed Will's face for the first time.

He had a split lip, a cut running through his left eyebrow, a bruise under his right eye, and a bruise along his jaw.

"Oh my God. Are you okay?"

He looked confused. "What do you mean?"

"Your face, you idiot. Sit down. Let me look at you."

Will blinked at me. "I don't—"

I grabbed him by the hand and led him over to his bed, making him sit so I could get a good view of the damage. I put a hand under his chin—gently, because of his bruised jaw—and tilted his head up.

He didn't pull away. He still looked mystified, but he sat perfectly still and let me examine him.

He'd obviously taken a shower after the game—his hair was still damp. The cut on his forehead was clean but it needed a bandage. The bruises looked painful and could use some ice. His split lip—

I raised my hand from his chin to his jaw, moving my fingers softly over the bruise there. Then I brushed my fingertips over his lower lip.

"This looks bad. Do you have Neosporin or something? And Band-Aids? This cut here needs a Band-Aid," I added, moving my hand to his forehead.

His auburn hair, fresh from his shower, clung damply to his skin. I brushed it back, and it felt so good against my fingers that I did it again.

His eyes widened, and I jerked my hand away.

"You look like you've been in a fight," I said.

He got to his feet again and shrugged. "It's nothing. Just game day stuff. My body's in worse shape than my face."

"What do you mean? What did you do to your body?"

"It's nothing," he repeated. "Seriously, par for the course. Football's a brutal game. I got off easy. One of the guys has a broken wrist and another one tore his ACL."

I stared at him. "And that's normal? Show me where else you hurt yourself."

"The trainers already checked me out," he said, but he turned his right side toward me and started to lift the hem of his shirt.

"Shit," he said almost immediately, wincing and letting the shirt drop. "Let's just leave it, okay?"

But I'd already seen the purple splotches, and I grabbed his T-shirt myself and lifted it.

It was the biggest bruise I'd ever seen, mottling his skin from his hip to his armpit. It looked worst right around his rib cage.

"Oh my God, Will. You're sure someone looked at this? You didn't crack a rib or anything?"

"No. It's just sore."

I let the shirt go and took a step back. "You should put some ice on that."

"I would, usually. But I was excited after the game and didn't feel like waiting around for an ice pack. I'm fine, Claire. I promise."

I'd forgotten all about the game.

"Oh man, I suck. I haven't even congratulated you or told you how awesome you were."

The side of his mouth that wasn't split lifted in a crooked smile. "Yeah?"

"Are you kidding? You were incredible. It was amazing to watch you."

"So you had a good time?"

"I did. I didn't expect to, but I really, really did." I paused. "You were right, you know. It was like a concert. The excitement . . . the feeling of being connected to all those people in the stands . . . and something wonderful happening in front of you." I paused again. "I'm ashamed I've never seen you play before. You heard my band so many times last year, and I didn't go to any of your games."

Will shook his head. "Like I told you before, I rode the bench last year. If I'd really wanted you there I would've asked—and you would've come." He grinned. "You came to this game, didn't you?"

Standing there in his white T-shirt and jeans, covered in cuts and bruises, Will was the picture of male strength. He looked like he'd been on a battlefield, coming home bloody but unbowed, his hard-muscled arms and powerful shoulders stretching the thin cotton of his shirt.

Of course, there were plenty of guys in the world with good bodies. There were plenty of guys who were good athletes. But not many of them had eyes like Will's, deep green and so full of warmth and humor and kindness . . . and now, pleasure in the fact that I'd come to his game and enjoyed myself.

It occurred to me that if I stayed in his room for too much longer, there was a really good chance I'd forget my pledge in a hot second and kiss him. But that would be reckless and impulsive and NOT something a good friend does. How could I be sure I was acting from real feelings for Will, and not out of my fear of being alone or my desire to be part of a couple again?

"Do you have any ice packs?" I asked abruptly.

"Yeah, downstairs in the freezer."

"I'll go grab them. You should ice those bruises."

Will shook his head and started for the door. "I'll get them. Do you want something to drink while I'm down there?"

"No, I'm good. But we need Neosporin and Band-Aids, too."

"Whatever I've got is in the bathroom."

Once he was gone it was like a weight lifted from my heart. Without those green eyes gazing into mine, I could remember all the promises I'd made to myself.

All I had to do now was figure out how to do that when he was in the room.

CHAPTER SEVEN

C oming down the stairs, I could see twenty or thir- ty people in the living room. It wasn't the crowd we'd had last time, but it was starting to look like a par- ty.

I went into the kitchen without stopping to say hi to anyone.

It was almost a relief to be away from Claire. The way she looked at me . . . the way she touched me . . .

"Will!"

I'd just grabbed the ice packs from the freezer. At the sound of my name, I turned around.

A girl I didn't recognize was standing in the door- way. Her Panthers T-shirt was a size too small for her, which sort of put a spotlight on her breasts. She had long blond hair a little darker than Claire's and blue eyes a little lighter.

She crossed the kitchen to give me a huge hug. Was it possible I actually knew this girl?

"I'm Brittany," she said, which probably meant I didn't.

The hug was over but she was definitely still in my personal space. She gazed up at me soulfully, which was a little embarrassing.

I'd had experience with the whole athletic fifteen minutes of fame thing back in high school. That was actually the reason Lissa first went out with me, even though our relationship turned into more than that. But after we broke up, I decided I wouldn't go out with another football groupie—and I wouldn't rely on football to attract girls.

Did that make me a hypocrite for being glad Claire was at the game today? Maybe. Probably.

But I was glad all the same.

"You were awesome today. Does this hurt?" Brittany asked, reaching out toward the bruise on my jaw. I jerked my head away, not wanting anyone but Claire to touch me like that.

"Sorry," I said. "It's a little sore."

"Of course," she said quickly, backing off a half step but keeping her eyes on mine. "Do you want any help with your ice packs? I could . . . you know . . . hold them on you."

There are some people who have the ability to make anything sound like a sexual invitation. Brittany was one of those people.

I felt my face getting red and I was glad no one else was around to witness my lack of coolness.

"I think I'm good," I said. "Maybe I'll see you later?"

"Count on it," she said, giving me a slow, very sexy smile.

I slipped past her and headed for the stairs.

Back up in my room, Claire was all business. She'd gotten a bunch of supplies from the bathroom and was sitting cross-legged on the bed.

"Let me start with your face," she said. As I sat down beside her, it occurred to me that if she'd said *Let me start by cutting off your left ear,* I would have gone along with that, too.

She poured hydrogen peroxide on a cotton ball and dabbed it on my forehead, and it wasn't the liquid that made my skin tingle. Then she opened the little tube of Neosporin, squeezed out a pea-sized dollop, and smoothed it gently over the cut.

Now it was more than tingling. I was practically shivering.

I couldn't look away from her face while she worked on me. She looked focused and serious, a single frown line between her eyebrows.

She didn't put peroxide on my lip but she did dab on a little Neosporin. Then she applied a small square bandage to the cut on my forehead and sat back in satisfaction at her handiwork.

"Okay, let me see the bruise on your side."

I pulled off my T-shirt obediently, wishing like hell I had a bruise lower down.

"Hold this," she said, putting one of the ice packs against my ribs. I kept it there while she wound a long strip of gauze around my waist to bind it in place.

"Good," she said, scooting back on the bed when she was done. "Keep that on for fifteen minutes, okay? And you should ice again before you go to bed. Oh, and you should take ibuprofen. It's good for pain, of course, but it's also an anti-inflammatory and will help control the swelling."

She shook out tablets from a bottle and handed them to me, along with a glass of water.

"Thanks," I said after I swallowed the pills. "If this is your bedside manner you're going to be a great doctor someday."

She grinned at me. "Well, I—"

There was a knock on the door. Before I could say anything it opened, and my new friend Brittany was standing in the doorway with another girl. This one was dark-haired and curvy, and her breasts, like Brittany's, were straining against the material of her Panthers T-shirt. It was just automatic when my eyes went there, and when I jerked my gaze back up to her face she was smiling.

"Hi," Brittany said cheerfully, glancing briefly at Claire before disregarding her completely. "This is my friend Nicole. We came to drag you down to the party. You *are* coming, right?"

A minute before, I'd felt like a million bucks. Maybe Claire really did have a magical healing touch, or maybe it was something else. But every second her hands were on my body felt like the best thing that had ever happened to me.

Now I felt pissed off and guilty at the same time, as if I'd been caught doing something I shouldn't.

I looked at Claire to see what she was thinking. Maybe I could figure out if she'd felt anything when she touched me . . . anything like what I'd felt for her.

But there was no conflicting emotion in her expression. She was just pissed.

She walked over to Brittany and Nicole and stood with her hands on her hips. "He'll be down in a few minutes. He has to finish icing his bruise first."

Brittany seemed pissed, too. "What are you, his nurse? Or his wannabe girlfriend?"

"Neither one," Claire said, grabbing the doorknob. "I'm just a friend. The kind of friend who thinks taking care of an injury is important."

She started to close the door, basically forcing Nicole and Brittany to back up or push past her. They chose to back up, and Claire shut the door in their faces.

Then she locked it.

"There," she said in satisfaction, turning to face me with her arms folded. "That should give you a few minutes of peace."

I looked back at her. She seemed so fierce and protective . . . even more now than when she was patching me up.

But was it the protectiveness a girl felt for a guy she wanted to be with, or the protectiveness a friend felt for another friend?

"Will," she said, sounding like she'd come to a decision.

God, I hoped it was the kind of decision I could get behind.

"Yeah?"

"I want to fix you up with someone."

I blinked. "What?"

She nodded several times. "Definitely. I mean, otherwise you're going to end up hooking up with someone like—" She gestured toward the door. "Someone who's only into you because you're a star quarterback."

Okay, that bruised my ego a little. "That's the only reason you could imagine someone being into me?"

She frowned. "Of course not. That's not what I meant. It's just that you should be with someone worthwhile. Someone who can appreciate all of you. Not just the football stuff and your—" Now she gestured at me.

I raised an eyebrow. "My what?"

She rolled her eyes. "Don't fish for compliments. Will you let me fix you up, or what?"

"I can find my own dates, Claire."

"You mean like those two Pantherettes?"

"They seemed like very nice girls," I said judiciously.

Claire glared at me suspiciously for a second, and then she relaxed.

"You're making fun of me."

"You're making it easy."

She leaned back against the closed door. "Yeah, okay, I guess I am. Sorry. Are you telling me it's none of my business?"

I shook my head. "I'm just telling you I can find my own dates."

"Fine. Just . . . not the Pantherettes."

"What if one of them turns out to be—"

"They won't."

"How do you know?"

"I just do."

I could have done more teasing on the subject, but the truth was, it made me happy that Claire cared enough to criticize two girls who'd flirted with me. I wanted to keep that feeling going.

"I don't want you to pick my next girlfriend, but you can tell me what you think about any prospective dates."

She looked skeptical. "How would that work? Will you be sending me their resumes?"

"We'll figure something out. Maybe you could casually stop by when they're here or something."

She chewed on her lower lip for a moment. "Do you have someone in mind?"

Only you, and that's not happening.

"No. But if I find someone I'm interested in you'll be the first to know."

She started to smile. "All right. It's a deal."

"Great. Now I'm going to take this ice pack off before I freeze solid. And then we're going down to the party. Apparently I have a flock of female admirers waiting to—"

"Admire you?"

"Exactly."

"Just remember you have to run any serious contenders by me first."

"I'll remember."

CHAPTER EIGHT

A few weeks after Will's season opener, Milton came up to me after band practice.

"You should think about writing some solo stuff," he said. "And performing it."

I frowned at him. "You don't like the stuff I've been writing for Sugar Lane?"

He sighed. "No, moron, that's not it. I've just been noticing something new in your lyrics. Your songs are getting more thoughtful, you know? I was just wondering if you'd ever thought about doing a coffeehouse-style gig sometime."

Milton was the least coffeehouse-style musician I knew.

"Is that an insult? Are you saying I'm not rock and roll enough?"

He mimed smacking me upside the head. "Will you cut that out? There's no subtext here. I'm not looking for a subtle way to say you suck. I think you're awesome. I was just noticing this other side to your style and wondered if you'd thought about exploring it. But I will never, ever bring it up again."

Later that night I was still thinking about what he'd said, and I called Jenna to talk about it.

My stepmother was always my go-to person for musical advice. She'd left home when she was seventeen to start a rock band, and she was still going strong almost twenty years later. I'd sent her a demo of Sugar Lane that she'd really liked, and she'd brought up the possibility of us maybe opening for the Red Mollies when they played a Boston club in February.

"Do you think I'm rock and roll?" I asked her.

"As opposed to what? Country? Maybe you're a little bit country *and* a little bit rock and roll."

"Very funny." I told her what Milton had said after practice that day. "I don't want to be some kind of folk singer. I don't see myself that way."

"You're nineteen," Jenna said. "You shouldn't see yourself any one way. You should be open to trying new things. Plus, all the great artists reinvent themselves on a regular basis. Sometimes they fail spectacularly, of course. But it helps them grow."

I felt a qualm. "I don't want to fail."

I hoped she'd say something comforting. Something like, *Don't worry, you won't.* But being Jenna, of course she didn't say that.

"You *should* want to fail."

"What?"

"Failure is important. It means you're taking risks. Isn't that what you wanted when you decided to be single for a while?"

I'd told Jenna about my pledge.

"I guess so." I was lying in bed, and now I closed my eyes. "If I'm being completely honest, I think I've been hoping there's a safe way to take risks. Which I know is stupid."

Jenna laughed. "Not stupid, just human. How's this for advice? Instead of worrying about the labels, just follow the music and see where it leads you. It sounds to me like that's what Milton was saying, too."

"All right," I said. "I think I can do that. Sometimes when I get an idea for a song, I—"

My phone vibrated. I opened my eyes and saw Will's name on the screen, and a little shiver ran down my spine.

There'd been two games since the season opener, one at home and one a few hours away in New York. I'd gone to both. We'd won both, too, and Andre had declared me the new team mascot, explaining that the only reason they'd lost so many games last year was that I hadn't been there.

Will and I had been hanging out a lot more, here at my dorm and over at his place. I felt like our friendship was on a really firm footing.

"I have to go," I said to Jenna. "Talk to you later, okay?"

Then I switched calls. "Hey," I said to Will, curling up on my side with the phone between me and the pillow.

"Hey. Still up?"

"No."

"No?"

"Well, I'm awake, obviously. But I'm in bed."

A beat went by. "Oh."

After that *Oh*, there was silence.

And then a rush of heat went through me.

I'd gotten pretty good at restraining my lustful feelings for Will when we were together. But I didn't have to restrain myself now, did I? I mean, he wasn't actually here. We were on the phone. He had no way of knowing that my whole body was now a few degrees warmer, or that my nipples tightened at the sound of his voice, or that there was an itch between my legs that made me squeeze my thighs together.

I let myself imagine that his next question would be, *What are you wearing?*

Nothing, I'd tell him, even though I was wearing a pajama top and underwear. Then he'd say—

"Are you still interested in hearing about my prospective dates?"

I was so caught up in my silly fantasy I didn't process what he'd said at first. "What?"

"You said you wanted to know about contenders. Girls I want to go out with?"

Well, that was one way to kill a girl-boner.

I sat straight up in bed. "There's a girl? A girl you want to go out with?"

I prayed to God I didn't sound as panicked to Will as I did to myself.

"Yeah. I met her yesterday at the gym."

"Why didn't you tell me about her yesterday?"

Now I hoped I didn't sound as pissy to him as I did to myself.

"I didn't know I wanted to date her yesterday. I mean, that only came up today."

I took a deep breath and tried to dial myself down a notch. "Oh." I cleared my throat. "So, tell me about her."

"Well, she's an athlete. A soccer player."

An athlete.

Before, the panic had been sort of amorphous. But now it was settling. Hardening.

An athlete. Will was a jock, and now he'd met a girl jock. They could talk about jock things in a way I couldn't.

I'd been thinking of the girls in Will's orbit as cheerleader types like the Pantherettes I'd met. But there were lots of other girls in his orbit. Girls who might not be interested in Will for superficial reasons.

Of course I didn't know this girl's deal. The mere fact that she was an athlete didn't mean she deserved an amazing guy like Will.

"Well." My voice was a little rough, and I cleared my throat again. "I need to meet her, obviously. You can't go out with her until I meet her. That's what we said."

"We did? I'm pretty sure you're making that up."

Of course I was.

"I want to meet her," I said stubbornly.

"I don't think there's time. Not before the date, anyway. We made plans already. Just now. She called me, and we're going out tomorrow night."

"Tomorrow night?" I could feel my panic rising again, and I forced myself to calm down. "Okay, how about this. Have her come to your house before the date, and I'll just happen to be there. You can be upstairs getting ready, and I'll have a chance to—"

"I already told her I'd pick her up at her place."

Of course he had. Will was the kind of guy who'd pick a girl up at her place. He was a gentleman, damn it.

"Unacceptable."

"But—"

"Nope. Unacceptable. Are you going to see her before tomorrow night? Is she in any of your classes? Will you run into her at the gym? I could be there working out or something and—"

I heard a snort of laughter. "You don't work out, Claire. You've never been in a gym in your life."

It was true. I'd told him that last year, and he'd offered to show me around the university fitness center and teach me to use the equipment.

Why, oh why hadn't I taken him up on that offer?

"Are you seeing her before the date or not?"

Now I definitely sounded pissy.

"Well . . ."

"You are. Where?"

"We're going jogging tomorrow morning before classes. But—"

"I'll come with you."

There was another silence, long enough for me to regret my impulsive and monumentally moronic offer.

"You want to come jogging with us? We're going to do five miles."

Was that a long way? I vaguely remembered running a mile and a half in junior high gym class, and it hadn't been that bad.

"Sure. I mean, running doesn't require any special skill. And it'll give me a chance to meet this girl and—what's her name, anyway?"

"Becky. But—"

"Becky. Okay. It'll give me a chance to meet her."

"Yeah, but I don't—"

"Do you not want me to meet her for some reason? Are you afraid I won't like her?"

"No, that's not it. I'm just not sure jogging is the best—"

"Just give me the where and when."

I heard him sigh. "Okay, but I'm going on record saying this is a bad idea. Do you promise you'll stop running if it's too much for you?"

The minute he said that, he pretty much guaranteed that I would run with the two lovebirds until I dropped.

"I promise," I practically growled. "Where and when."

"The lake on the north side of campus. We're meeting in front of the science building at six."

"Six a.m.?"

"Yeah. But if you don't—"

"I'll be there. Good night, Will."

"Good night."

I tossed my phone onto the nightstand and ran my hands through my hair.

Six o'clock in the morning. I was going on a five-mile run at six in the freaking a.m.

I flopped back down on the bed and stared up at the ceiling.

What had I gotten myself into?

CHAPTER NINE

I set my alarm for five a.m., but by the time I stopped hitting the snooze button it was five-thirty.

I jumped in the shower for a quick rinse, mostly just to wake myself up, and then I put on a pair of black yoga pants (the closest thing I had to athletic gear), my sturdiest bra, and a gray Hart University T-shirt. I added a headband to hold back my hair and my black Chuck Taylors, which were the only sneakers I owned.

I was worried I'd be late if I walked, so I drove my car to the science building parking lot.

I was five minutes early, but Will and Becky were there before me. They were stretching together, using one of the iron benches scattered along the lake path for balance, and I saw them before they saw me.

Becky wasn't gorgeous, but she was pretty. She had brown hair in a ponytail, thick dark eyebrows, and a long, lean, strong-looking body.

She and Will had their left legs up on the back of the wrought iron bench and they were stretched out over their thighs, their heads turned toward each other as they chatted. They both looked a lot more serious about the jogging thing than I did with actual running outfits (Becky's was purple) and actual running sneakers (Becky's were neon green).

I slowed down as I approached them. The sun was just beginning to come up, and the scene in front of me was spectacular.

The early-morning mist on the lake was touched with red and gold. There were geese on the water floating silently by. The sky was a clear, transparent blue and the trees lining the lake path were moving softly in the breeze.

Set against that background, Will and Becky looked sort of perfect together—happy and healthy and athletic, like they were about to film a Nike ad.

Standing there in my yoga pants and T-shirt, with my music geek sneakers and black socks—I didn't own any white sports socks—I felt like an interloper.

They still hadn't seen me. If I turned around now I could leave before they knew I was there. I could send Will a text to explain that I—

"Claire!"

Will straightened up and waved, and I forced a smile onto my face as I closed the remaining distance between us.

"Hi," I said, looking at Becky. "I'm Claire."

"Becky. It's so great to meet you. I saw your band last spring at the student center. You guys were amazing."

She liked my music? Damn.

"Thanks. I, um, hear you play soccer."

She nodded. "We're having a great season this year, but you'd never know it." She sent a mock glare Will's way. "Considering that all the money and attention go to football."

Will grinned. "Hey, I'm with you on this. I know it's not fair. But that article you wrote was great, and if people keep speaking up maybe things will change."

"Article?" I asked.

Will nodded. "Becky covers sports for the Hart Star. She wrote a pretty tough piece on college athletics, showing the disparity of resources between men's and women's sports."

She was a feminist? Damn.

Once again, I considered bagging out. I could tell them I had a headache or a stomach ache or a leg cramp or—

Becky moved closer to Will and bumped his hip with hers. "Are you ready to go?"

It wasn't a big deal. One little hip bump. But something flared up inside me, and when Will said he was ready I said, "Me, too."

"Great. It's two and half miles around the lake, so we'll do two laps."

I nodded. "Two laps. Great."

Will spoke up. "You can stop after one, you know. And let us know if you need to slow down the pace or—"

"I'll be fine," I said quickly.

Will looked like he wanted to say something else, but then he just shrugged. "Okay."

The first section of the path was wide enough for the three of us to run side-by-side. We started off at what seemed like a pretty reasonable speed, and I felt confident that I could keep it up for two laps.

I continued to feel that way for about a minute and half.

After ninety seconds, I was panting and wheezing. My leg muscles were burning and there was a stitch in my side.

Will and Becky were having some kind of fitness geek-out about aerobic and anaerobic exercise and target heart rates. Becky had a Fitbit and she was telling Will how much she loved it. I was trying to shore up my determination to keep going when Will asked me a question.

"What?" I gasped out.

"I said, can you talk? That's a good test to make sure you're not exercising too hard."

If that was the case, then Will was doing fine. He wasn't having any trouble talking. He might as well have been sitting down.

I took a few deep breaths and made a mighty effort.

"Yes, I can talk. Don't worry about me."

Two sentences without a huff or a puff. Yay Claire.

Will took me at my word and he and Becky went back to their conversation. I didn't even try to listen to what they were saying, focusing all my energy on moving my arms and legs. When the path narrowed, I gratefully dropped behind the other two.

"How are you doing?" Becky asked me over her shoulder, her voice as unstressed as Will's and her smile sweet and friendly.

I hated her.

I marshaled another massive effort. "I'm great."

After that things were a little easier. The two athletes were ahead of me, so at least I didn't have to worry about them seeing my red face and the ever-increasing pain and agony in my expression. And they couldn't hear my heavy breathing, either.

As we kept going on the path to hell, I focused on Will. He was like a machine, his legs pumping like pistons, up and down, up and down, as measured and tireless as pile drivers.

My eyes shifted over to Becky. She matched him stride for stride, her legs as piston-like as his were. And it was obvious from the way she was talking that this wasn't even a stretch for her.

She was probably taking it easy because of me.

They probably both were.

The insanity of what I was doing swept over me. What had I been thinking? How could I have thought, even for a second, that going on a five-mile run with two jocks was a good idea?

They were both so healthy and strong, so vibrant and glowing. A sudden image of the two of them in bed together filled my mind.

They'd make love with all the gusto and vitality they were currently displaying. And then, after all the wild, gymnastic sex, they could head to the kitchen to make postcoital spinach smoothies.

Was that a thing? Spinach smoothies?

What the hell did I care. It was the sex part that bothered me.

Because I was jealous. Obviously.

Jealousy had dragged my aerobically-challenged ass out of bed at five-thirty in the morning. Jealousy had started me on this hellish journey around a lake I now loathed. Jealousy might actually end up killing me, since there was a good chance I would drop dead any second now.

On and on it went. Out of some misguided sense of something or other I refused to stop, pushing myself further and further until—

"Claire?"

Will had turned his head a few times to check on me, and I'd managed to smile and offer a few words as proof of life. This time, though, he figured out I wasn't doing so hot.

He stopped in his tracks and I did, too, never more grateful for anything in my life as the simple cessation of movement. I couldn't hide the fact that I was gasping for breath, and I knew I was tomato-red and not in an attractive way.

Sweat was pouring down my face. We'd stopped near one of the iron benches, and Will grabbed my hand and led me over to it.

"Shit," he said, looking worried. He had a water bottle attached to his belt, and now he pulled it loose and handed it to me. "Here."

I took a sip but I felt nauseous on top of everything else, and I was afraid if I drank too much I'd puke.

"You're overheated," he said, making me sound like a car engine. He knelt down in front of me, his handsome face so sweet and concerned I wanted to cry.

Now Becky pulled out her own water bottle. "You should pour this over your head," she said, sounding as concerned as Will did. "That will cool you down."

Maybe it would, but it would also render my humiliation complete. "No, that's—"

"Good idea," Will said, taking the bottle from Becky.
He raised it over my head, turned it upside down, and let
it gush.

I'd never experienced such a total dichotomy. The
water felt wonderful on my body—glorious, even. But
the utter humiliation of this moment seemed to wither
my heart until it could have blown away like a dried leaf.

Dramatic much?

Yep. But as I sat there with water dripping into my
eyes and soaking my clothes, I'd never felt such overwhelming despair.

I used the back of my hand to wipe my face.

"Okay, thanks. I'm good now. Why don't you guys
finish your run and I'll—" I gestured back toward the way
we'd come. "I'll go back."

Will was still kneeling in front of me. "No way. We'll
go back with you."

At that moment, I would have done anything to keep
that from happening. Trudge back to my car soaking
wet with Will and Becky hovering solicitously? Oh, hell
no.

I shook my head. "I'm fine. Really. You guys go on
and I'll—"

"I'm going back with you. This whole thing is my fault. I knew you weren't a runner and I still let you come."

Just when I thought I couldn't sink any lower. "Will, please. Please. I want to go by myself, okay?"

"We haven't come that far. Just let me—"

Instinct made me turn toward Becky. "Please. I'll be fine. I want you and Will to finish your run. Please?"

I'm not sure how much Becky understood about how miserable I was or why, but she gave me the help I needed.

"Do you have your cell phone with you?"

I nodded.

"All right. Let's go, Will. Claire will call us if she needs anything. Right, Claire?"

"Yes. Absolutely." I made a shooing motion with my hands. "Go, run, be free."

Becky put a hand on Will's shoulder. "Come on."

"All right." Will rose reluctantly, his face unhappy as he looked down at me. I smiled as cheerfully as I could and made the shooing motion again.

"I'll see you later," I said, even though, at that moment, I was planning to crawl into a hole and pull it in after me—and never face Will again.

Finally they left. I watched them until they were out of sight—man, they were in good shape—and then I slumped down on the bench and stared at the lake.

The mist was gone now, but it was still peaceful. It was so silent, in fact, that I could hear my heartbeat still thundering in my ears and the harsh rasp of my breathing.

I sat there for a good five minutes. I would have stayed longer, but I was afraid I might run into Will and Becky back at the science building if I didn't head back soon.

So I dragged my sorry ass off the bench and plodded back the way we'd come.

CHAPTER TEN

I worried about Claire until we finished the first lap. When I saw that her car was gone from the science building parking lot, I knew she'd made it back okay.

Becky was the perfect jogging partner. She kept pace with me, she was fun to talk to, and she obviously loved running as much as I did.

I just hoped she couldn't tell that my mind was on Claire when it should have been on her.

Once the run was over I did my best to refocus. "So, tonight. I'll pick you up at seven?" I asked while we were doing our post-run stretches.

"Sounds great."

If dinner went well, I'd be kissing Becky good night in about fifteen hours. If the kiss went well, maybe she'd invite me into her apartment.

Lissa was the first and only girl I'd been with. How was I supposed to know if I was a good kisser, or if Lissa and I had just been used to each other? What if I was a bad kisser?

What if I was bad in bed? What if—

Becky had said goodbye and started to leave. Now she stopped, came back, and pressed a quick kiss to my cheek.

"See you tonight," she said, flashing a brilliant smile before turning away again.

I sank down onto the bench and stared after her.

Once she was around the corner of the science building and out of sight, I let go of the breath I hadn't realized I was holding.

Becky was nice, and I liked her. She wasn't beautiful like Claire, but then no one was. Lissa wasn't beautiful, either, but I'd loved the way she looked and I was definitely attracted to her.

I was attracted to Becky, too. Wasn't I?

The touch of her lips hadn't thrilled me the way the touch of Claire's fingers did, but that didn't mean I wasn't attracted to her. Claire seemed pretty well committed to her singlehood pledge, and I'd decided I'd better make peace with that fact if I didn't want to start mooning around writing poetry about unrequited love.

Then, when I'd made the date with Becky, Claire was the first one I told.

Was that because we were getting to be really close friends? Or because a part of me hoped she'd be jealous?

This morning's run had shot that theory all to hell. No girl who liked a guy would go for a run she wasn't in shape for and let herself get all blotchy and sweaty.

Of course Claire probably had no idea that when her face was red and glowing all I could think about was making her come, and wondering if she'd look like that afterward.

I sighed. Time to forget about the girl I couldn't have and think about the girl who might actually want me.

* * *

I took Andre's advice and dressed up that night, wearing khakis and a button-down shirt.

"In the current climate of casual sex and hookup culture," he'd said, imitating our psych professor's pedantic delivery, "a girl will appreciate a little retro courtship. Do it up right, man."

I'd also taken his advice about the date itself, making a reservation at a restaurant downtown.

Becky lived in an off-campus student apartment building. I got there at six-thirty, realizing after I found a parking place that I couldn't show up at her door half an hour early.

Okay, no big deal. I'd just wait in the car.

I watched the traffic going by for about ten minutes. Then I pulled out my phone and texted Claire.

I'm supposed to pick Becky up at 7. I got here early and I'm sitting in my car. I'm nervous as hell and I feel like an idiot. Help.

I sat and stared at my phone, waiting for her response.

It came after a minute.

What are you nervous about? That girl's crazy about you.

She was?

I started typing again.

Why do you think that?

I only had to wait ten seconds this time.

Are you kidding? She hip bumped you this morning.

That was true. I remembered it. And she'd kissed me on the cheek. But—

That doesn't mean she's crazy about me.

Oh, please. Any kind of touching at this stage is a sign. But hip to hip? Dude, that's below the belt touching. Very close to the danger zone. SHE WANTS YOU.

When Claire texted in all caps, I could visualize her talking—her arms and hands getting into the action. When Claire was excited or emphatic she talked with her whole body. She was like that on stage, too.

I grinned as I typed my response.

Maybe you should come with me on this date to translate the body language. I obviously don't have a clue.

That's what makes you adorable. Don't worry. You'll be fine.

Claire thought I was adorable?

What if I'm not?

OH MY GOD. Just get out of your car and go. You can be a few minutes early.

I checked the time; eight minutes till seven. If I walked slow I'd be at her door right on the dot.

Okay. But keep your phone close just in case.

Just in case what? You need me to rescue you? Forget it, buddy. I'm already in my pajamas and I'm not leaving the dorm tonight. I have a hundred pages of biology to read.

I pictured Claire curled up in bed with a textbook.

I won't ask you to leave the dorm. But what if I need advice?

During your date? What are you going to do, text me under the table? Here's some advice: DO NOT DO THAT. I'm signing off now. Good luck and have fun, you goofball.

I smiled as I slid my phone into my pocket. Then I got out of the car, took a deep breath, and went to knock on Becky's door.

* * *

An hour or so later, Becky and I were at the restaurant. We were finishing our salads when her phone buzzed. She looked at the screen and made a face.

"Do you mind if I go outside and answer this? It's my dad."

"No, of course not. Take your time."

I waited until she was out of sight and then I pulled out my own phone.

Are you there?

The response came almost immediately.

Yes, I'm here. How's it going? Please tell me you're not texting under the table.

I smiled.

No, she had to take a call from her dad. She's outside right now. It's going OK, I guess. But our conversation's a little boring. If I'm bored, doesn't that mean she's bored?

Not necessarily. What have you guys been talking about?

Classes. Movies. It's me, isn't it? I'm boring.

No you're not! Don't be silly. Maybe get a little more personal? Ask something revealing. Or tell her something revealing.

Like what?

I don't know. What are you most afraid of?

I didn't have to think about that one.

Fire.

You're afraid of fire? I didn't know that.

Not fire in general. A fire. My house burned down when I was a kid.

OMG. Was anyone hurt???

No, we were all fine. But if I have a nightmare that's what it's about.

Do you have a lot of nightmares?

Not anymore. None at all for the last year.

That's good. I'm glad.

I wasn't sure what to say next. Apparently Claire wasn't, either.

After a moment I started typing again.

What are YOU most afraid of?

Several seconds ticked by, and I started to wonder if she might not answer.

Being alone.

That answer surprised me so much that I didn't respond for a minute. Then:

You're not alone. There are so many people in your life who (my finger hovered over the L key before moving to the C) *care about you.*

I know. It's not rational. Fears aren't, right? But that's the reason I want to be single for a while. I don't want to start seeing someone just so I won't be alone. I don't want to be afraid of being on my own. I want to conquer this fear.

You're on your own tonight.

True. Or at least, I would be if you'd go back to your date. Good night, Will.

Good night.

I slid my phone into my pocket and leaned back in my chair.

Becky came back a minute or two later, just as the waiter brought our main courses. It was an Italian place and we'd both ordered pasta.

"Sorry about that," she said as she took her seat.

Maybe this was a chance for us to get a little more personal.

"Is everything okay?" I asked.

She shrugged. "More or less. My parents are divorced and they split game days. My dad was supposed to come tomorrow, but he wants to trade with my mom for next week instead. Sometimes they put me in the middle of their battles."

She didn't seem upset, but the scenario she'd described didn't sound fun.

"That must be rough on you."

She shrugged again. "I don't let it get to me. It's not something I can control, right? So I don't take sides and I tell them to work it out between them."

I was impressed. "Wow, that's mature."

"You sound surprised."

"I guess I am. I mean, you're my age, right? Nineteen?"

She grinned. "Actually, I'm twenty," she said, swirling her fork in her pasta. "So maybe that explains it."

"It can't always have been easy though, right? The thing with your parents. How old were you when they divorced?"

"Sixteen. But it's not a big deal. Seriously."

She seemed serene about it all, and it occurred to me that she always seemed serene. Of course I didn't know her very well. Maybe she got more animated the better you knew her.

Not that there was anything wrong with being serene.

We finished our main courses. We had dessert. I gave the waiter my card for the bill, and while we were waiting for him to come back Becky went to use the restroom.

The moment she was gone, I pulled out my phone.

I'm not feeling it.

What?

This date. Becky. I'm not feeling it. What do I tell her?

Why do you have to tell her anything? Thank her at the end of the night and don't go out with her again.

But she's expecting sex.

Expecting sex? WTF? What do you mean?

She told me her roommate won't be home tonight "in case I want to stay over."

Whoa. What did you say?

I mumbled something.

Will.

I know, I know. But she caught me by surprise. So what do I do? She'll be back soon so type fast.

Five seconds. Ten seconds. Then:

I've only had the one boyfriend and he broke up with me so I don't have a ton of experience with this. BUT Tamsin once told me a good way to end things with someone. You say, I had a great time with you tonight, but I don't feel enough chemistry to take things further.

I thought about it. Then I typed:

That's actually kind of brilliant. It makes it not about the person, right? And it's true. I think she's great, but I'm not feeling the chemistry. That's exactly the situation.

There you go then. Good luck.

Thanks.

I slid my phone back into my pocket just as Becky came back.

"Ready to go?" she asked.

I nodded.

Ten minutes later we pulled up in front of her apartment building. I walked her upstairs to her door, and while she was fishing in her purse for her key, she said something about going running before breakfast tomorrow.

I cleared my throat. "Becky."

She smiled at me. "Yes?"

"I, uh, had a great time with you tonight. I'd love to go running with you tomorrow or anytime. But I don't feel enough chemistry to, uh, take things further."

What had sounded so sensible in Claire's text and in my head now sounded too formal. But it was out there, and all I could do was wait for her response.

Her eyebrows went up.

I held my breath.

"Wow," she said. "That's really kind of . . . respectful."

I breathed out again.

"Seriously," she said. "I mean, a lot of guys would sleep with me first, you know? And then just not call." She paused. "I like this better."

"Well, I like you." I was feeling so relieved it made me like her even more. "And I'm serious about the jogging thing. Do you want to go running this weekend?"

She nodded. "I'd like that. Maybe Sunday?"

"Yeah. Sunday."

She stuck out her hand. "Thanks for dinner, Will."

We shook hands solemnly. "Anytime, Becky. Good night."

"Good night."

I called Claire the minute I was back in my car. "It worked."

"It did? That's great!"

"I know." I paused. "It's not that late. Do you mind if I stop by? I won't stay long."

A beat went by. "Um, sure. Of course. I guess I'll see you in a few minutes?"

"Yeah."

CHAPTER ELEVEN

I wasn't sure exactly why I'd invited myself over like that. But when I opened Claire's door and saw her sitting on her bed, her biology textbook beside her and her guitar in her lap, I knew why.

Claire was the person I always wanted to see.

"Hey," I said.

"Hey."

"I like your pajamas."

I really did. They were covered in Winnie-the-Pooh characters—the classic drawings, not the Disney versions.

She set her guitar on the floor and looked down at herself. "I've had these forever." She looked back up at me. "You're a cross between Pooh and Tigger. On the Winnie-the-Pooh personality scale."

"I am?" I wanted to sit on the bed with her, but I grabbed her desk chair instead. "Well, you're pure Tigger."

"No way. I'm Piglet. Or at least that's how I feel most of the time."

"You feel like a Very Small Animal?"

She nodded. "I'm afraid of so many things. And I'm always hoping someone will come along and protect me."

Let me be the one who protects you. From everything. Forever.

"But that's not what you really want?" I asked slowly.

She shook her head. "I want to learn to protect myself." She was sitting cross-legged on the bed, and now she looked down, her right index finger tracing one of the Tiggers on her pajama bottoms. "That's why I—"

"Made your singlehood pledge?"

"Yes."

Was that her way of warning me off? Or just a friend sharing with another friend?

Whichever way she meant it, I had to take it to heart.

I changed the subject. "You're not Piglet on stage, you know. It's Tigger all the way when you're singing."

She looked up again, smiling. "Really?"

"Definitely."

She shifted position, wrapping her arms around her shins and resting her chin on her knees. "So here's the chicken and egg question. Is the Tigger side of me my true essence, or is that just a costume I put on when I perform?"

"True essence," I said without hesitation. "But that doesn't mean you're not Piglet, too. People are complicated. You said I'm Tigger and Pooh, right? So why can't you be Tigger and Piglet? And Piglet's not a coward," I added. I dug into my memory. "Remember when Pooh writes that poem to celebrate how heroic Piglet was during the storm? And Piglet isn't sure he deserves the poem, because Pooh said that he never blinched, and in reality he did blinch. And then Pooh says, 'You only blinched inside, and that's the bravest way for a Very Small Animal not to blinch that there is.'"

Claire looked at me. "You can quote from *The House at Pooh Corner*?"

"My mom read Winnie-the-Pooh to me every night for years." I paused. "Does that cost me manhood points?"

"Are you kidding? It makes you adorable." She shifted again, sitting back against her headboard. "Your mom raised you right. How long was she on her own? If you don't mind me asking," she added quickly.

"No, I don't mind. Brian—my biological dad—never wanted anything to do with me. My mom raised me by herself until I was fifteen. Then Alex—my stepdad—came into the picture. He's actually Brian's half brother," I added.

Claire's eyes widened. "Really? That sounds . . ." She searched for the right word. "Complicated?"

"Not really. I mean, if Brian were still in the picture it might be. But he's not a part of my life and never has been. But Alex . . ." I shook my head. "He's the best man I know. He was in love with my mom forever, since they were in high school together. He played football in college and in the NFL before he started coaching. He moved back to Weston—that's where I live, in Ohio—to coach my high school football team."

"And then he and your mom fell in love?"

I remembered what those first few months had been like and I smiled. "Not exactly. They fought all the time. Then the fire happened."

"When your house burned down?"

I nodded. "Alex offered to let us stay with him while we figured things out."

"And *that's* when they fell in love."

"Yep."

"How did Alex propose? Were you there?"

I grinned. "My mom proposed to him, actually. I was in the hospital when they told me they were getting married."

"The hospital? Why were you in the hospital?"

"I was knocked unconscious in a game. I had a concussion."

"Oh, wow. Isn't that kind of serious? I mean, is there a risk with you still playing?"

"No. I didn't have any after effects or anything like that."

"Your mom and Alex seem really nice. And really happy together."

I remembered that Claire had met them during our season opener. "They are. Sickeningly happy, actually. But my mom deserves to be sickeningly happy for the rest of her life."

"That's how I feel about my dad."

"When did he meet your stepmom?"

"I was fourteen."

"Your parents weren't together?"

"They got divorced when I was three." She hesitated. "My mom died in a car accident when I was eleven."

My heart squeezed in my chest.

"I didn't know that. I'm so sorry."

She nodded. "It was rough. And my dad and I had a rough time together, after that. I didn't live with him. I lived with my grandparents. Then, when I was fourteen, I was visiting him over the summer and, well, Jenna happened."

"Jenna 'happened'?"

Claire grinned. "Yep. That's kind of how Jenna is. She happens. She came into our lives and . . . I don't know. Woke us up? I moved back in with my dad, he and Jenna fell madly in love, and they got married."

"And you like her? As a stepmom, I mean?"

"I love her. She's my role model. Whenever I think I can't be alone—whenever I feel like I want to rush into a relationship—I think about her."

Another reminder that Claire didn't want to be with me. Not right now, anyway.

"Why do you think about her?"

"Because she was alone for a long time, and happy. She took care of herself, you know? She started a band when she was younger than me."

"The Red Mollies, right? I didn't realize they've been together for so long."

"They weren't. I mean, they broke up for a few years. They got back together around the time Jenna married my dad."

"Huh. Do you ever think about being in a band? Not just on the side, but as your career?"

Claire hugged her knees again. "Not really. I mean, I've wanted to be a doctor for a long time. My dad's a heart surgeon."

"Is that what you want to do?"

She shook her head. "I want to be a pediatric oncologist."

I stared at her. "Kids with cancer? That's a really rough gig."

"I know. But it's rougher for them, right?"

A rush of feeling started in my heart and spread to every part of me.

"You're going to be an amazing doctor."

She looked doubtful. "Even though I have so much Piglet in me?"

"*Because* you have Piglet in you. You understand what it's like to be a Very Small Animal. To be afraid and keep going anyway."

She hugged her knees tighter. "That's a really nice thing to say, Will. Thank you."

There was a pause. And the longer the pause went on, the more I wanted to walk over to Claire, pull her into my arms, and kiss her until she forgot everything but me.

And yet, that's exactly what she didn't want. She didn't want to lose herself in someone else.

She wanted to be on her own.

We spoke at the same time.

"I should probably—"

"It's getting kind of—"

We stopped.

"I should probably go," I said.

"It is getting kind of late," Claire said.

I got up to leave.

"Thanks again for your help tonight."

"Anytime. Just consider me your personal dating guru, always willing to go above and beyond."

That reminded me of the run with Becky.

"Shit, I forgot about this morning. How are you feeling? Are you sore?"

She nodded. "The next time I need to meet a prospective date of yours, can we do it over coffee or something? I took a forty-five minute shower this afternoon and my muscles still hurt."

I didn't need the image of Claire standing naked under a flow of steaming hot water. For a moment I forgot what I was doing. How to form words. How to think.

"So . . . good night," Claire said after what might have been five seconds or five minutes.

"Good night," I said quickly. Then I got the hell out of there before the rush of blood to my crotch could become a hard-on—a raging hard-on that Claire would definitely notice.

I'd turned down sex with Becky to spend time with the girl I burned for . . . and would probably never be with.

It was looking like a night for me and my right hand.

CHAPTER TWELVE

A few weeks later, the Panthers were getting ready for a game in Ohio.

"That's too far for me," I said. I was hanging out at Will's house the Wednesday before the game, sitting at the kitchen table.

"Come on, you have to go." That was Tony, one of Will's housemates, who was at the stove with an old-fashioned popcorn maker. He hated microwave popcorn and refused to allow any in the house.

"You're our good luck charm," Delford added as he dug into a bag of pretzels.

He still wasn't my favorite guy in the world, but he didn't wear his asshole T-shirts when I was around. Andre said I was a good influence, and I hoped to use my powers, such as they were, for the greater good. If I could encourage Del to be less douche-y the public at large would benefit.

I shook my head. "You guys don't need me to win. You're strong on both sides of the ball, and your cornerbacks are the fastest—"

"Whoa." Will was on the other side of the table working on an English essay, but now he closed his laptop and stared at me. "When did you start talking like an NFL analyst?"

I looked down my nose at him. "I've been to all your games, I pay attention when you guys talk, and ESPN is always on over here. Plus, your mom's been giving me pointers."

"Whoa, whoa, *whoa*. You're talking to my mom? When did that happen?"

"We follow each other on Twitter. We tweet back and forth during your games."

Will covered his face with his hands. "My mother is on *Twitter*? My God, that's like a sign of the apocalypse or something."

"Your mom's awesome. And that's another reason why you guys don't need me at this game. It's just an hour away from your house, right? Your mom and Alex will be there. That's all the good luck you need."

Will opened up his laptop again, but he glanced at me before he got back to work. "It won't be the same as having you there."

Tony and Delford had started a conversation about superheroes—Flash vs. Arrow, it sounded like—while

Will and I had been talking about his mom. Now, when he spoke that last sentence, his voice was lower than it had been. Private.

Intimate.

In the next moment he was back to work, focused on his computer screen and his essay. Maybe I'd just imagined that feeling of intimacy, that look in Will's eyes.

I'd been getting that look from him a lot lately. Just hints of it, brief moments . . . but still.

There was no question we were friends. Really good friends. I felt like I could talk to him about anything, and I knew he trusted me, too.

But there was one thing that we didn't talk about. A kind of unspoken tension humming below the surface.

Except that, because we didn't talk about it, I couldn't really be sure it was there at all.

Maybe it was all in my head.

He never made an actual move or anything like that. He never did or said anything to make me uncomfortable. He knew about my singlehood pledge, and he seemed to understand why it was important to me.

After his dinner with Becky—even though it hadn't turned into anything—I'd figured he was going to start dating on a regular basis. But that dinner had been three weeks ago. Since then, nothing.

Was it possible that he was . . . well, waiting for me?

Every time the idea occurred to me I squashed it. How conceited was I to even think something like that? How many nineteen-year-old guys would be willing to wait for a girl?

And yet . . .

What if he was? Did I want him to?

No.

Maybe?

No.

But . . .

And so my thoughts went, around and around like a hamster in a cage.

I'd thought that being single this semester would make everything easier. Simpler. And in some ways, it had. But why did my emotions seem more complicated than ever?

I decided to put it out of my mind for tonight. I needed to head back to my dorm soon anyway, so there was no use in worrying about it right now.

The sound of popping corn got intense, and in a minute Tony took the canister off the heat and poured the fluffy white kernels into an enormous bowl. He'd melted an entire stick of butter in the microwave, and after drizzling that slowly and evenly over the popcorn he added salt and mixed it all together.

"Okay," he said in satisfaction. "Time for the crossover episode. Popcorn and beer in the living room. D, would you grab the six pack from the fridge? Will, call it quits for the night. Your paper's not due till Friday. Claire, are you staying?"

"What crossover episode?"

"Flash and Arrow."

That's why they'd been arguing the merits of the two heroes. "I should be heading back to Bracton. I have an early class tomorrow."

"Oh, come on," Will said, closing his computer again. "You can stay for an hour. You know you love Tony's popcorn."

It was true. I did.

Plus, my heart beat a little faster when Will coaxed me.

"All right," I said. "I'll stay for the show."

We settled down in the living room. Del was on the armchair, Tony and Will were on the couch, and I was on the floor in front of Will with my legs stretched out.

It was a good episode, but after the first five minutes I barely noticed what was going on. That's because Will had leaned down during the first commercial and said, "You keep rolling your shoulders. Do you have a crick in your neck?"

"Yes, but it's fine. I slept funny last night."

"Lean back," he said. "I'll give you a massage."

"That's all right. I—"

He didn't bother to argue the point. He just put his big hands on my shoulders and got to work.

The next half hour was ecstasy . . . and torture. Will seemed to know exactly where the knots were, and exactly how to work them out. The feel of his hands—not just touching but kneading, stroking, caressing—sent ripples of pleasure through my body.

I never wanted him to stop. And yet I was conscious of Del and Tony, fearful that they would guess what I was feeling and exchange the kind of knowing looks that would put air quotes around my "friendship" with Will, as though it were nothing more than foreplay for what every girl *really* wants.

A relationship.

But Del and Tony weren't paying attention to us at all. They'd gotten into a discussion about the scientific feasibility of time travel in the Marvel and DC universes, and they decided they needed to refer to Del's extensive comic book collection for information. They headed upstairs, arguing all the way, and suddenly Will and I were alone.

I was leaning back against the sofa in front of him. His long legs were on either side of me, which meant if I leaned my head back I'd touch his—

Shit.

I stayed frozen in place, not sure what to do. The lights were off, and the only illumination in the room came from the big TV.

I stared at the screen as though I were fascinated, even though I couldn't have told you what was going on to save my life.

Behind me, all around me, I could feel Will's warmth and strength. And running underneath that melody was a deeper, darker beat of sexual energy that enveloped me like a mist.

I closed my eyes, trying to get a handle on myself. And then:

"How does that feel?"

I could feel his breath against the back of my neck, and I shivered. He must be leaning forward. How easy it would be to turn my head and kiss him. To fall into his arms. To take him by the hand and drag him upstairs to his bedroom.

Somehow, some way, I found the strength to scoot away from those incredible hands and scramble to my feet.

"That was awesome," I said, trying to sound normal and cheerful and not like a woman whose panties, I just now noticed, were wet.

Oh, God.

"Thank you so much," I went on, going over to the table where I'd left my backpack and turning on a lamp for good measure. "I feel a million times better."

"You're going?"

I glanced back at him. He looked good enough to eat sprawled out on the couch, his auburn hair tousled and his green eyes hooded.

"Yep, I think I should. I've got an early class tomorrow. Like I said."

"You can stay over if you want." One side of his mouth went up. "We know we can share a bed without anything happening."

I remembered the morning I'd woken up in Will's arms, and I knew if that ever happened again there was no way, NO WAY, I wouldn't tear his clothes off and have my way with him.

"I think I should spend the night in my own bed. But thanks."

"Anytime."

My heart was in knots and my body was aching, overheated, restless.

"I've got a lot of work this week and a gig to practice for. You guys are leaving for Ohio on Friday, right? So I probably won't see you till you get back on Sunday."

Will nodded, and I couldn't tell what he was thinking. "Are you going to watch the game?"

"Is it on television?"

"There's a live stream thing happening at the campus center."

"Oh. Then yes, I'll be watching."

"Okay. Good."

I made it to the front door without giving into my urge to launch myself onto the sofa, and I only turned back when my hand was safely on the knob.

"Good luck at the game, Will."

"Thanks. I'll see you on Sunday, Claire."

There was an undercurrent to his words that made my heart pound. A kind of . . . purpose.

What was he planning to do or say on Sunday?

I had no idea. But I'd better be ready for anything.

* * *

I ended up watching the game in Dyshell's room with Tamsin. Dyshell had a huge computer monitor, so it was like watching the live stream on TV. Dyshell and I were on the bed while Tamsin was curled up on Dyshell's bean bag chair.

At the end of the first quarter the game was tied 7-7. During the commercial break before the second quarter I asked Tamsin,

"So. How are you doing with the, uh, pledge?"

She looked at me with her eyebrows up. "Are you implying I've fallen off the wagon?"

"No, not at all! But if you have it's okay," I added quickly.

Dyshell grinned at me. "How are *you* doing on the pledge? I hear you and Will are getting awfully . . . cozy."

I forgot sometimes that Dyshell had a spy on the inside—her brother Andre.

Tamsin sat up straight. "Wait a sec. You and Will?"

"No," I said firmly. "Definitely not." I paused. "But let's say, for the sake of argument, that I'm tempted."

Tamsin put her elbows on the bed and rested her chin in her hands. "Go on."

I cleared my throat. "I asked you first," I said primly. "I mean . . . have you been tempted this semester?"

"You want to know the truth?"

I nodded.

"I haven't."

Dyshell and I both stared at her.

"Seriously? Not once?" Dyshell asked. "You haven't gotten drunk at a party and wanted to make out with some guy?"

Tamsin spread out her hands. "Hey, I'm as shocked as you are. I think part of it is that I haven't been partying as much this semester. I mean, that was on purpose. I figured it would be easier to resist temptation if I didn't deliberately put myself in situations where my willpower would be compromised, you know?"

I thought guiltily of all the time I spent with Will. "I know."

"I'm actually really happy so far. I'm not planning to join a convent or anything, but I think a semester . . . or even a year . . . of celibacy will be good for me. It's kind of good to think about other things, you know? I'm going to audition to play Beatrice in *Much Ado About Nothing*. I've never tried Shakespeare before."

"That's great, Tamsin," I said, trying to sound enthusiastic. In my heart of hearts, I'd been hoping she'd admit to wanting to end the pledge . . . so that I could think about ending it, too.

Of course Tamsin's not an idiot.

"Claire, you don't need my permission to fall off the wagon if you want to. It was nice to have company at first, but it's something I'm doing for myself now. The whole point of it was to be stronger and happier, right? If being with Will would make you happy, then that's what you should do."

My shoulders slumped. "But that's the problem," I said. "I don't know if it would make me happy. I mean, I'm enjoying being single, too. But then I think, what if he meets someone else and I miss my chance? And *then* I think, what if we get together and it's terrible? Or what if it's awesome first and *then* turns terrible, like with Ted? If we break up we won't be friends anymore. Are you guys friends with anyone you've broken up with?"

They both shook their heads, and Dyshell put her arm around my shoulders. "But that doesn't mean—"

I interrupted her. "And what if we have a real chance for something special? If we get together too soon we'll screw things up."

"You broke up with Ted two months ago," Tamsin pointed out. "Isn't that a long enough mourning period or whatever? Aren't you past the rebound danger zone?"

I thought about that. And then something else came to the surface, something I'd been thinking about for a while.

"I don't want to set a time frame before I can be with someone else," I said slowly. "I mean, I don't want it to be like being in a couple is the default setting and the time between relationships is just a placeholder." I paused. "Being single can be its own setting. Can't it? Jenna is totally happy with my dad, but she loved being on her own, too. She says she learned things about herself she wouldn't have any other way."

I took a breath. "I want to know who I am without setting my clock by a guy. Do you know what I mean? With a guy, getting over a guy, about to be with a guy."

"I get that," Tamsin said.

I was on a roll now. "I've been writing a ton of new songs. The band is sounding really tight. My grades are up, and I know it's because I'm not spending all my time on the phone with Ted or thinking about Ted or crying about Ted or sexting with Ted. We were together for four years. Being his girlfriend was a huge part of my identity for a really long time. I'm just thinking it would be easy to drift into that again, you know? And I don't want to."

Dyshell nodded. "That makes a lot of sense. But not all relationships are the same, are they? Isn't it possible that being with the right person could, I don't know, affirm you instead of erase you?"

Tamsin rolled her eyes at that. "Not any relationship I've ever been in."

"Well, but isn't that—"

She didn't have a chance to finish. The commercial break ended, and Dyshell and I both forgot everything else as our beloved Panthers lined up for the first snap of the second quarter. Tamsin would probably have preferred to continue the conversation, but she knew it would be hopeless until the next commercial.

"Will looks good today," Dyshell murmured as he cocked his arm back to throw a pass, cool and confident as he scanned the field.

"I know. The team brought in a new quarterback coach who really—"

Then, out of nowhere, a linebacker broke through the offensive line and laid Will out flat.

The world stopped spinning.

My breath stopped. My heart stopped. I waited in frozen terror for Will to get up from the brutal hit . . . only he didn't.

"He's unconscious," I gasped. "Oh my God. Oh my God."

I grabbed Dyshell's arm. Tamsin came to sit on the bed with us, her face drawn and tense.

Wake up wake up wake up wake up wake—

There was a crowd around him now, so thick I couldn't see him clearly. The team doctor, coaches and trainers, and of course the players. The announcer was saying the obvious—*the Panthers quarterback appears to be unconscious*—and I gripped Dyshell so hard it must have hurt her.

I remembered the first episode of *Friday Night Lights*, when the quarterback of the—oh my God, the Dillon *Panthers*, was that a sign?—made a tackle after an interception and ended up paralyzed.

How long would it take me to get to Ohio if I started driving right now? Could I afford to fly?

But no, I was being crazy. I'd been thinking of Will as far away, but actually he was only an hour from his hometown. His parents were in the stands. He didn't need me.

Then they brought a stretcher onto the field, and I felt sick.

"What's happening? Oh God, what's happening?"

But nobody could answer me.

CHAPTER THIRTEEN

Ten days later, Will came back to Hart.

I hadn't talked to him at all. Not even once. I'd texted him, emailed him, and left voice mails, but he hadn't texted or emailed or called me back.

After a few days I stopped reaching out, figuring he'd get in touch with me when he was ready. It was hard, though. I didn't want to bother him when he was recovering from a concussion, but I was desperate to hear his voice.

I was getting news from Andre and from Holly, although I tried not to ask for updates too often. I didn't want to bug them, and I didn't want to seem pathetic . . . especially since Will obviously didn't feel a burning need to communicate with me.

I was having trouble sleeping. Lying awake at night, I found myself wishing I'd given in to my longing for Will before he'd gotten hurt. If I were his girlfriend, I'd have some kind of standing, wouldn't I? He'd have to talk to me.

His family had standing. His teammates had standing. His coaches and doctors had standing. Maybe some of his non-football friends had standing, but if so, I wasn't one of them.

It hurt more than I could bear, and on so many different levels. Will was in pain—physically and emotionally—and I couldn't do anything to help.

I'd heard a few days before, from Andre, that Hart's athletic department had barred Will from playing football again. Apparently this was his third serious concussion—I remembered him telling me about the one he'd had in high school—and the second time he'd lost consciousness.

As the days went by with no word from Will, I started to research concussions. What I learned terrified me. Repeated head trauma could lead to something called CTE—Chronic Traumatic Encephalopathy—which was, essentially, irreversible brain damage. Professional athletes—football players and boxers, mostly—who suffered from this kind of trauma developed symptoms that resembled early onset Alzheimer's along with chronic head pain, troubles with balance, vision, and cognition, and severe depression.

These athletes also committed suicide at alarming rates.

Will wasn't an NFL player who'd endured tens of thousands of blows to the head over a long career. But he'd been playing football since he was a little boy, and he'd had three serious concussions already. In addition to that, according to one medical journal article I read, it was likely he'd suffered hundreds of subconcussive events—blows to the head that weren't diagnosed as concussions but which, over time, contributed to long-term damage.

After I read all that, I was grateful that the Panthers had barred Will from continuing to play football. But I doubted very much that Will was feeling the same way.

I was sure his mother had told him his health was a million times more important than football. But I wanted to add my voice to hers, and to the voices of the doctors and others who were telling Will it wouldn't be safe to risk more head trauma. I wanted him to know that his friends cared about his life and health more than anything else.

That they cared about *him.*

It was Andre who told me Will was back at Hart, and that he'd be going back to class in a few days. I sent a short text—*So glad you're back, please call when you can*—and then waited exactly forty-eight hours to see if he'd get in touch with me.

Crazy scenarios started running through my head. What if he'd actually forgotten who I was? Amnesia could sometimes result from head trauma. But surely if he had something as serious as amnesia, the doctors wouldn't clear him to return to class?

Unless it was partial amnesia, which—

Which was the stupidest idea I'd ever had. Selective amnesia? Will could remember everything in his life except for me?

Finally I couldn't take it anymore. No longer caring if I seemed pathetic—or even if I *was* pathetic—I texted Andre.

Has Will mentioned me at all?

The response came within a minute.

Not yet. But he's coping with a lot right now.

I knew that, of course. But that was the point. I wanted to help. I needed to help.

The next afternoon, after my last class, I headed to Will's house.

I'd chosen this time of day deliberately. His housemates would be at football practice, which meant that Will, if he was home, would be there alone. Sure enough, when I pulled up in front of his place, Will's car was the only one in the driveway.

The front door wasn't locked. I opened it as quietly as I could, and saw right away that the living room was empty.

So was the kitchen. If Will was here, he was up in his room.

Halfway up the stairs, I heard his voice. I could hear Holly's voice, too, so she was either on speaker or they were Skyping.

Will's bedroom door was ajar. I stopped in the hallway and waited for their conversation to end.

"But *why?*" Will was saying. "Three concussions and out isn't some kind of rule. Not every college does that. The NCAA doesn't have any guidelines on how many concussions you're allowed to have. I've been talking to people at other schools, and if I get a second opinion from another doctor I can transfer and play somewhere else. Maybe even at a higher-profile program. Scouts have been watching me play, mom. I've been having the season of a lifetime, in case you didn't know. Do you really want me to throw that away?"

"As opposed to your life?"

Holly sounded angry, frustrated . . . and scared.

I could sympathize.

"Will you cut that out? Those aren't the only options. It's not a choice between quitting football and dying."

"That's not what Dr. Pitney said."

"One doctor! That's what I'm saying. If every doctor in the world gave me the same advice, then fine. But I guarantee you that if I saw a hundred doctors, ninety of them would say I could keep playing."

"And I'm telling you that I don't care! When it comes to your health, which side of that argument do you think

I'll choose? If it was one doctor against ninety-nine, which side do you think I'd choose?"

"But it's my life! Not yours. If it's a risk, then it's my risk to take."

"There's no guarantee the risk will pay off. You know the odds against playing professional football."

"Of course I know. But even if I only get to finish out my college career, I still want to play. I want to play for as long as I can. Why don't you understand that?"

"Because I'm your mother! Because I don't want you to die, or suffer the long-term consequences of repeated head trauma! Do you think I could stand to see you knocked unconscious again? Wheeled off the field on a stretcher, while I sit in the stands wondering if you're alive or dead? Why don't *you* understand *that*?"

"It's my life! *My* life! You can't just take football away from me. It's not fair."

"I don't care if it's fair. I'm telling you no. You're not getting a second opinion. You're not transferring to another school. And that's final."

There was a brief moment of silence. Then a sudden, loud crash and Will's voice.

"Fuck!"

Had he fallen? Was he hurt?

I dashed across the hallway and pushed the door open.

Will was standing in the middle of the room, his hands on his head. The lamp beside his bed was lying on the floor, the ceramic base cracked and the bulb broken. Beside the bent lampshade I saw his cell phone. Will had thrown it with enough force to knock the lamp from the night stand.

I must have made a noise—a gasp or something—because Will spun around and saw me. He stared, and I stared, and neither one of us said a word for what felt like a long time.

I was shocked. Hearing the rage in his voice a moment ago and seeing the wild fury in his eyes now, I almost didn't recognize this Will as the Will I'd known for more than a year.

After a minute I couldn't stand the silence anymore. I couldn't stand feeling like I was with a stranger. I wanted Will to speak, to reassure me he was the same person he'd always been.

"Hey," I said, my voice sounding shaky. "It's good to see you."

CHAPTER FOURTEEN

Of all the people I didn't want to see right then, Claire Stone was at the top of the list.

I'd lost football. The thing that had defined me for more than half my life. The one thing I could do better than most people. The thing that had made Lissa fall for me, and that I'd hoped might help Claire fall for me, too.

Now what did I have to offer? Football was the only thing that had made me special. I didn't know who I was without it. Even last year, when I rode the bench, I'd thought of myself as a football player first and a student second.

I'd lost my athletic scholarship. My mom and Alex had told me over and over again that they could afford my last two years at Hart, but they weren't rich and I knew tuition would put a strain on their finances.

My one chance to get everything back was transferring to a school that would let me play. There were plenty of them out there.

But my mother refused to even consider it. I got the sense that Alex was more open to the idea, but there was no question he'd defer to my mom on this one.

Of course I was nineteen, so theoretically I could do what I wanted. But that would mean going against my mother—the one person who'd sacrificed for me my whole life. How the hell could I do that to her?

So now here I was, between a rock and a hard place. I had headaches no pain reliever could touch, and bright lights were still my enemy. I'd let down my teammates and my coach. And if I somehow managed to achieve my best case scenario—convincing my mom to let me transfer to another football program—I'd still have to leave my friends and the team I loved . . . and Claire.

Seeing her was suddenly unbearable.

"Get out," I said. "I don't want to talk to you right now."

Her head jerked back as though I'd slapped her.

"I just . . . wanted to be sure you were okay. You didn't, um, answer my texts."

I knew I hadn't. I'd saved them all, along with her emails, and for a few days I'd read them over and over again. I'd listened to her voice mails over and over, too.

Then, after Hart made its final decision about my football career, I'd deleted everything.

"I have a lot to deal with right now. In case you didn't know," I added, which was a shitty thing to say.

Her hands squeezed into fists. "I know. Of course I know." She hesitated. "On my way up, I heard you talking with your mom. It sounds like you, um, want to transfer to another school? Where they'll let you play football?"

I shrugged. "Yeah. But my mother's not down with that plan."

She looked at me with those big blue eyes, and I almost broke down and begged her forgiveness for being an asshole. Then she said:

"I know you don't want to hear this right now, but Holly's right. Your life and your health are more important than football. I've been reading about athletes and concussions and—"

My head started to throb. "Jesus Christ. You're not a doctor yet, and you're not my mother. I don't need a lecture from you. Just get out, okay? Get the fuck out."

Claire's face turned bright red. She took in a deep breath and let it out slowly, as though she was trying to keep herself from crying.

"I'm sorry," I said gruffly. "I just—" I shook my head. "It's not a good time, okay? Seriously, Claire . . . you should go."

"Isn't there something I can do to help?"

She took a step toward me, and I took three steps back. If she touched me it would all be over. I'd fall apart or cry or some shit, and there was no way I was letting that happen.

"You could sleep with me, I suppose. I could stand to burn off a little steam."

She froze. Her eyes turned bright, and in the next instant there were tears trembling on her lashes. She blinked, and I saw one tear slip down her cheek before she turned and fled.

A few minutes later I was lying on my bed, my forearm over my eyes.

"What the fuck did you do to Claire?"

It was Andre. I let my arm drop to my side so I could look at him. He was standing in the doorway like a mountain of righteousness, and I'd never felt myself wallowing so deep in wrongness.

"She just showed up, man. I didn't ask her to come here. I wasn't in the mood to see anyone, so I sent her away."

Andre took three long steps into the room and stood there glowering at me. "Claire isn't just anyone. That girl has been worried sick about you. She's been asking me every day—every hour, sometimes—how you are. If there's something she can do to help. She cares about you, you asshole. And whatever you said to her had her crying her eyes out. She wouldn't tell me what happened, probably because she knew I'd tear into you if she did. You hurt her, and the only thing she cares about is protecting you."

Guilt washed over me, but I hardened my heart against it. If I let anything but anger in I'd fall apart.

"Good for her. Look, I've got a headache. Just leave me alone, okay?"

* * *

Going back to class was harder than I would admit to anyone. Loud noises and bright lights still bothered me, looking at computer screens bothered me, and even though I was downing Advil and Tylenol like candy, the headaches were sometimes so bad I'd sit in the lecture hall with my eyes closed and my hands pressed to my temples, just waiting for the pain to go away.

Eventually it did. Two weeks after I got back to Hart, the headaches started to get better. I was feeling less foggy in the mornings, too.

The only thing that wasn't getting better was my mood.

The shittiest thing I'd done was not apologizing to Claire. I'd thought about it a hundred times. I'd written a hundred different texts and deleted them all without sending.

I'm sorry I was such a jerk.

Please forgive me.

And most pathetic of all:

I miss you.

But I knew if I made any kind of overture, she'd be with me in a heartbeat. And I still couldn't stand the idea of seeing her. Not when my life was so fucked up . . . and not when I was still trying to convince my mom to let me transfer.

If I had my way, I'd be leaving Hart. So what good would it do to patch things up with Claire? That would only make me want to stay—and torture me with what I couldn't have.

I had enough of that in my life already.

I still thought Alex was my best bet for talking sense into my mom. As November went by I started to feel better—physically, anyway—and I talked to Alex almost every night. I told him about the players I'd spoken to at other schools, and whatever I'd read that day on the internet that bolstered my case. Alex didn't argue with me; he mostly just listened. I thought that was a good sign until I made an all-out pitch the Monday before Thanksgiving.

"I'm flying home on Wednesday," I reminded him. "I thought you and mom and I could sit down then and talk about this. I've put together some information that should calm her down. Stuff from medical journals and doctors about—"

"Will."

I had a feeling I wasn't going to like whatever he was about to say. "Just listen to what I—"

"It's not going to happen."

My heart sank. If Alex wasn't on my side . . .

"But you haven't even heard me out yet. You haven't—"

"Will, I've been listening to you for the last month. I've been listening to you, and to your mother, and to the sports medicine doctors I've called personally."

Shit.

"But—"

"Will, I love you. And I understand in my gut how you feel about football, because I feel the same way. I told myself I would keep an open mind about your injury because that's what I would've wanted people to do for me when I was a player. And I have kept an open mind. So when I tell you this, it doesn't just come from the love I feel for you as your stepfather. It also comes from the advice and opinions of medical experts I trust, and from my instincts as a coach. You shouldn't play football again, Will."

Ever since the injury on the field, the blows had kept coming. This one, though, felt like the knockout punch.

"I don't have to do what you say." My voice trembled like a little kid's, and I hated myself for that. "I'm nineteen years old."

"I know. I guess that's a decision you'll have to make for yourself. You'll have to decide who you trust, and who has your best interests at heart."

My own heart was a raging mess. I knew that my mother and Alex loved me. Of course I did. But I also knew that I loved football, and that I didn't want to let it go without a fight.

I knew something else, too. I knew there was no way I could go home for Thanksgiving without saying things I'd regret—and maybe some things I wouldn't be able to take back.

"I'm not coming home."

"What?"

"On Wednesday. I'm not coming home."

Silence. Then:

"Your mom and I will come to you, then. You shouldn't be alone on Thanksgiving."

The swirl of anger and pain inside me was getting worse every second.

"You guys can come out if you want, but I won't be here. I'm going to take a road trip and think things through. I'll call you next week."

I ended the call before Alex could say anything else, and then I turned off my phone so I wouldn't know if he tried to call back.

The truth was, I had no intention of taking a road trip. I would stay here, although if my mother and Alex made an appearance I would definitely take off.

So what did I want to do over the holiday break? Just about everyone I knew would be gone.

Get drunk, I decided.

And after that?

I'd see where the spirit took me.

CHAPTER FIFTEEN

I got a call from Andre on Tuesday night. After we finished talking, I sat cross-legged on my bed and stared at my phone for a long time.

Then I went to Julia's room to ask her for a really big favor. Once we figured out the details, I called my dad.

"I have something to tell you that you're really, really going to hate."

"That sounds ominous."

"I can't come home for Thanksgiving this year."

"Okay, you're right. I really, really hate that." He paused. "You have three minutes to make your case."

I took a deep breath. "You know everything that's been happening with Will?"

"Yes."

"Well, he's in a bad place. A monumentally bad place. I'm scared to death for him, Dad. I just talked to Andre, and apparently Will's decided to stay here over the break. Alone. And if he spends the week the way he's spent the last two days—"

"How has he spent the last two days?"

"Drinking."

"Damn. I don't need to tell you how stupid and dangerous that is, on a lot of levels. He's underage, he had a serious concussion not long ago, and—"

"I know, Dad. That's why I want to stay. We're going to do an intervention."

"Who's 'we'?"

"Will's friends. Some of us, anyway."

I could hear my dad's sigh all the way from Iowa. "That's something his parents should be doing, sweetheart."

"If he was going to listen to his parents, I wouldn't be talking to you about this."

"I know you mean well. But, Claire—"

"Maybe no one can get through to him right now. Maybe we won't be able to help. But we have to try. And, look. I have his mom's phone number. If there's anything we can't handle, I'll call her. All right?" I paused. "But I don't think I'll have to. Will's a wonderful, incredible person. Underneath all the stuff he's going through right now, he's still a wonderful person. I just want to remind him of that." I paused again. "Please, Dad. Please. I'll make it up to you and Jenna over Christmas, okay?"

He pounced on that immediately. "Does that mean you'll stay with us for the whole break? You won't spend two weeks in Boston like you were planning?"

I sighed. "Fine."

"All right, then. You can spend Thanksgiving at Hart helping your friend. But if anything is off, anything at all, you'd better call his folks like you said you would—and you'd better call me, too."

Relief spread through me. "I will. I promise. And, Dad? I love you."

I already had my bag packed for my trip home, so I didn't have to waste time on that. I left the dorm, tossed my suitcase into the trunk of my car, and drove to the bar Andre had called from.

Del was waiting for me out front.

"Will's inside with Andre and Tony," he said. He looked worried, which was disconcerting. Del never worried about anything.

"I'll wait here for you guys," he said, sticking his hands into his pockets. "I'm not that good in a crisis. This is more Andre's scene."

I found them in a booth way in the back. The bar was dark and seedy and smelled like cheap beer and air freshener, and it struck me as exactly the kind of place you'd expect to serve an underage kid carrying a fake ID.

I slid into the booth beside Will and across from Andre and Tony. Will had his head buried in his arms and he was snoring loudly.

"How many drinks did he have?"

"Five," Andre said.

I looked at Will, sprawled out over the scarred wooden table with his head in his arms and peanut shells stuck in his hair. It looked like he hadn't shaved since yesterday.

"Five drinks did that to him? He's such a big guy."

"I know, but he's not usually much of a drinker. He doesn't have a tolerance built up or anything."

I dug into my mental files for some of the info I'd looked up after Will's injury.

"People can be more sensitive to alcohol after a concussion." I frowned. "I bet his doctor told him that at some point. I bet he knows he shouldn't be drinking."

Tony was looking frustrated. "Of course he knows. But he's not in a mood to listen to reason."

Andre nodded. "I guess he had a bad conversation with his folks or something. Anyway, that's when he decided not to go home for Thanksgiving—and when he started drinking. He skipped his classes today, too."

"Okay." I leaned across the table to emphasize my next point. "If this plan is going to work we have to be all in. Are you sure you and Dyshell can make it out to the cabin tomorrow night? There's no way I can do this alone."

"We'll be there," Andre said. "We already cleared it with our parents. Coach won't let me off practice tomorrow, but after that we'll hit the road."

Tony was looking at a weather report on his phone. "It's supposed to snow tonight. Where's this cabin again?"

"Out in the Berkshires," I told him. "I saw that report, too, but they'll have the roads plowed by tomorrow afternoon."

"What about you?" Andre asked. "Will you be okay?"

I nodded. "Julia said it's a two hour drive. If I start now I should beat the snow."

"Okay. Let's get him into your car."

Andre and Tony got Will on his feet. Once we were outside, Del helped, too. Between them they got Will to my Corolla. He was only half awake, and he didn't offer much resistance when his friends stuffed him into my passenger seat and belted him in. Once that was done, his eyes closed and the snoring began again.

"He might puke at some point," Del cautioned me, as one who knows of what he speaks.

"This car's pretty ancient and it's been through a lot. We can both take it." I paused. "At least with a guy you don't have to hold back his hair."

I got into the driver's seat and rolled down my window when Andre knocked on the glass.

"Call me if you have any problems."

"I will. Rikki and Sam are coming out tonight if the roads aren't too bad. Otherwise, they'll come with you guys tomorrow." I glanced over at Will. "He's not going to give me any trouble. He'll be sleeping it off."

"Okay. Is your phone charged up?"

"Yes."

"All right. Have a safe trip."

"Thanks, Andre. See you tomorrow."

The snow started sooner than I'd been expecting—about twenty minutes into the trip, when I still had an hour and a half to go. For most of that I'd be on the Mass Pike, which was a major road and felt safe. After that, once I got on the back roads, I'd just have to grit my teeth and get through it.

I would've thought it was beautiful if I hadn't been the one driving. I love snow, and—from the passenger seat—I love the way the flakes hitting the windshield look like stars flashing by on an intergalactic journey. But I was behind the wheel, which meant I was responsible not just for my safety but for Will's. So it was hard to enjoy myself.

It wasn't bad at first. The snow didn't even stick for the first twenty minutes. After that I moved into the far right lane, slowed down to thirty miles an hour, and felt grateful for the taillights of the car in front of me.

According to Siri I was about five miles from my exit when the car I'd been following fishtailed and ended up on the shoulder.

I was afraid if I braked I'd skid, too, so I kept going past. The car hadn't crashed into anything, so I figured they'd be okay.

I hoped I'd be able to say the same thing about Will and me.

"In a quarter mile, take the exit onto Wintervale Road."

Thanks, Siri.

Cars were becoming few and far between and the visibility was terrible. I slowed down to a crawl for the exit, seeing with dismay that this road hadn't been plowed at all yet. Praying that I wouldn't run into too many hills—in spite of the fact that I was now in the Berkshire Hills—I shifted into first gear and drove very, very slowly through the thick layer of snow.

There were hills, of course.

I skidded coming down one and almost didn't make it up another, but I came out okay—mostly because there wasn't a single other vehicle in sight for me to crash into. Everyone else was obviously too smart to be out driving in what was turning into a heavy snowstorm.

Finally I made my last turn onto a dirt road surrounded by trees, and Siri informed me that my destination would be on the right.

My stomach was in knots and every muscle in my body ached with tension. What should have been a two hour drive had turned into four.

Will had slept through most of it, the lucky bastard, although he'd woken up twice. The first time he'd mumbled something indistinct before going back to sleep. The second time he'd said, very clearly, "Bruce Springsteen and the E Street Band," which I felt I could disregard under the circumstances.

As I pulled into the driveway of the cabin that belonged to Julia's family—they'd given us permission to use it over the holiday weekend—Will was still snoring, though more quietly than he had been before.

I decided to leave him in peace while I took a look at the cabin. Julia had told me what to expect, but what if the storm had knocked out the electricity? That would mean no light and, more importantly, no heat.

Which would really, really suck.

But once I unlocked the front door and used my phone's flashlight to find the light switch on the wall, I was relieved to discover that the electricity was working just fine.

Halle-frickin-lujah.

The cabin was lovely, although I'd probably appreciate it more under different circumstances. There were floor-to-ceiling windows along one wall and a fireplace along another, with a big stack of firewood beside it. In front of the hearth was an oriental rug and an enormous leather couch, well worn and very comfy-looking, and two equally cozy-looking armchairs. The walls were painted cream with slate blue trim and there were black and white nature photos everywhere.

The downstairs was an open design, with the kitchen and dining area visible from the living room. A wide staircase led upstairs where, Julia had told me, there were three bedrooms.

I found the thermostat and turned on the heat, grateful to hear a furnace grumble to life somewhere. Hopefully it wouldn't take too long for the house to warm up.

Outside, the wind had picked up and the snow was coming down thick and heavy. As I trudged through the six inches already on the ground, I felt stupid. Why hadn't I taken the weather reports more seriously?

Because a storm this early in the season was unusual, that's why. I hadn't really believed the predictions.

I didn't even have my winter coat. It was hanging in my closet back in Iowa, and I'd been planning to pick it up over the break. I was wearing my warmest jacket, but even so, I was shivering by the time I got back to the car.

Will was still asleep in the passenger seat.

Damn. What if he wouldn't wake up? There was no way I could manhandle him the way Andre and Tony had. He outweighed me by a hundred pounds.

But when I opened the passenger door and shook him by the shoulder, he opened his eyes and stared at me.

"What the hell?" he asked, his voice gravelly from alcohol and dehydration.

"We're here," I said, pushing the button to release his seatbelt. "Let's get inside."

Will swung his legs around and started to get out. When he noticed the swirling snow for the first time, he stopped.

"How long was I asleep?" he asked, sounding bewildered. "Where are we?"

Both fair questions.

"We're at Julia's family's cabin in the Berkshires," I explained.

He stared at me like I was nuts. "What are you talking about?"

"I'll explain it to you when we get inside."

His brown leather jacket was even lighter than mine, and when a strong gust of wind blew snow into his face he shivered.

I pointed toward the house. "The front door's open. I'll be right behind you."

I waited a few seconds to make sure he headed in the right direction, and then I got my bags out of the trunk and followed him.

Once we were both inside I closed the door behind us. Even though the house was still cold, it was a relief to shut out the storm.

Will was standing with his hands on his hips, looking around. Then he turned to face me.

"Claire, what the fuck is going on? I feel like I'm in the twilight zone."

When I'd first come up with this plan, and when I'd talked it over with Julia and Rikki and Andre, it had seemed like a good idea. But now, having driven hours through a snowstorm to a remote cabin and standing face to face with a very confused, very pissed off Will, it seemed like a less good idea.

I cleared my throat. "This is an intervention," I said.

CHAPTER SIXTEEN

My head was still spinning and my mouth tasted like a toilet. I would've thought I was dreaming if I hadn't felt so shitty.

"An intervention? Jesus Christ. What are you talking about?"

Claire stood there in her puffy blue jacket with her face pink from cold. There were snowflakes on her hair and eyelashes.

"An intervention," she said again, like that would explain everything. She brushed the snow off her jacket and went over to the big couch. "Come sit down."

I followed her, but only because I needed to find out what the hell was going on. If it weren't for that, I would have stayed as far away from her as possible. I had a feeling I was about to be more pissed at Claire than I'd ever been at a human being in my life.

I sat down on one of the armchairs, wishing like hell there was a fire in the fireplace.

"It's freezing in here," I growled.

Claire was sitting on the couch, looking small and fragile inside her puffy jacket.

"I know," she said, sounding apologetic. "The heat's on but I'm not sure how long it will take to warm up."

She looked as cold as I felt. And no matter how mad I was, I couldn't just sit there while she was shivering.

There was wood, kindling, newspaper, and matches beside the fireplace. I got up from the chair, checked the flue, and started gathering what I needed to make a fire.

"Can I help?" Claire asked behind me.

I didn't even turn to look at her. "No."

In a few minutes the twisted newspaper and kindling were ablaze on the hearth, flames licking at the bigger logs I'd stacked in the andirons.

Just the sight of the fire made the air feel warmer, and once the big logs caught I held my cold hands out to the blaze.

I saw out of the corner of my eye that Claire had come to sit beside me on the rug.

"That feels wonderful," she said, holding her hands out like I was.

We sat there in silence for a minute. Then, confident that the fire wouldn't go out, I went back to the armchair, moving it closer to the fireplace before sitting down again.

"Okay," I said. "It's time to explain what the hell we're doing here."

Claire stayed where she was, taking off her jacket and sitting cross-legged a few feet from the fire. She was wearing a dark blue sweater and jeans, and with her blond hair and pink cheeks she looked like an ad for a ski resort.

"Andre called me from the bar," she said.

The bar?

Oh, right. The bar.

Slowly, my fuzzy memories began to knit themselves together.

"He was worried about you," Claire went on. "He said you've been drinking the last few days." She paused. "All your teammates are worried."

A hot pulse of anger turned my hands into fists. "They are, huh? That's sweet. Did Andre happen to mention that most of those guys drink ten times as much as I do?"

"That's why they're worried. You're not acting like yourself. You don't even sound like yourself anymore."

I looked into the heart of the fire. "I'm not myself anymore. I'm not a football player."

Claire scooted across the rug until she was only a foot or so away. "Come on, Will. You know there's more to you than football."

"Yeah. A guy who drinks too much, I guess."

Claire frowned. "You shouldn't be drinking at all. Alcohol is a neurotoxin. Your body treats it like a poison, and while it's getting the alcohol out of your system it slows or stops your recovery from the concussion."

I used to think it was adorable when Claire talked like the doctor-to-be that she was. But right now, it pissed me off.

"I'm recovered. The doctors cleared me. I don't have headaches anymore."

Not as often, anyway. And not as bad.

Claire shook her head. "Recovery from a concussion can go on for months. Alcohol can only slow that process down. People who've suffered brain injury are more sensitive to alcohol, and alcohol can magnify the physical and cognitive problems of TBI."

Now she was talking in acronyms. "What the hell is TBI?"

"Traumatic Brain Injury. Another thing is, you're about eight times more likely to suffer from depression in the first year after TBI. And since alcohol is a depressant drug, using it can cause or worsen depression."

"I'm not depressed."

"Really? Then why are you drinking, Will? Why did you go to that bar?"

The fire was really going now. My back still felt cold but my face and chest were warm.

"Because I wanted to get drunk."

Claire shifted her position, drawing her legs up and hugging her knees. "Is that all?"

I shook my head. "I picked that bar because it's got a reputation, and I wanted to get into a fight. After that, I was hoping to hook up with some girl and have a one-night stand."

One of the logs split, falling off the andirons in a shower of sparks.

"Will."

I hated the sympathy in her voice, and I hated how pathetic I felt.

"Shit," I said. "I wanted to get drunk and throw some punches and have anonymous sex, and just look at me now. I'm not even good at being bad."

"That's why I love you," Claire said. She paused, and then added, "That's why we all love you."

I closed my eyes. I thought of all the times I'd imagined Claire saying those words to me, and then I thought about how I looked—and smelled—right now.

Like crap.

Not that it mattered, of course. Claire loved me as a friend, and she'd dragged me out here for the same reason. Which reminded me—

"Why the hell are we here? Have you taken me prisoner or something?"

That made her smile. "It's an intervention, like I said. We decided to spend Thanksgiving break with you. Trying to convince you not to flunk your classes or drink yourself into oblivion or whatever."

"I see. So where's the rest of my therapy circle?"

Claire looked embarrassed. "Okay, so, it's possible I didn't plan this very well. I also should've paid more attention to the weather reports. Rikki and Sam were supposed to come out tonight, but that obviously won't be happening. Andre and Dyshell and Tamsin and Julia are supposed to come tomorrow."

"Why aren't you guys spending Thanksgiving with your families?"

"We decided this was more important. We're going to have Thanksgiving dinner here. With you. Tamsin and Julia are going to shop for a turkey and all that before they come out, and we're all going to do the cooking."

I felt a little shaken. My friends had sacrificed Thanksgiving at home to be with my sorry ass?

But I shook off the guilt and went back on the attack. "I didn't ask you guys to do that."

"I know. We—"

All of a sudden, I needed to get away.

"I feel like shit and I smell like shit. Does this place have a shower?"

Claire scrambled to her feet. "I'm sure it does. Upstairs?"

I wanted to find more reasons to be mad. "I don't suppose your brilliant plan included bringing along a change of clothes for me?"

Claire looked stricken. "I didn't think of that. I'm sorry." Then she brightened. "But Julia said there are sheets and towels and things here, so maybe there's other stuff, too. She has two brothers. Maybe they left some clothes. Let me go see what's in the bedrooms."

She took off before I could say anything else, and I watched her hurry up the stairs until she was out of sight.

While she was gone I put another log on the fire and nudged the others with a poker. I knelt down on the hearth and stared at the blaze until the heat became too intense.

I got to my feet and backed away just as Claire came hurrying back downstairs with something in her arms.

"Okay, I found a few things in the bedroom at the top of the stairs. A pair of jeans and some shirts and a pair of pajamas. I laid the clothes out on the bed but I brought these down."

She handed me what she'd been holding—a pair of men's pajamas, white with navy blue pinstripes.

I took them from her and shook out the bottoms, holding them up to my waist. The pant legs ended about three inches above my ankle.

"They're a little small," I said.

Claire bit her lip. "I'm sorry."

She really did look sorry, and God knew she had plenty to be sorry for. But as I stood there facing her I realized I was bone-tired, and I didn't have the energy to rub anything in her face at the moment.

"It's fine," I said. "I'm going to go take a shower."

Claire's tense face relaxed a little. "Okay. Good. I brought some food, and Julia said there's canned stuff and staples in the kitchen. I'll make us something for dinner."

The thought of food made me feel nauseous. "That's all right. I'm not really hungry."

Then I brushed past her and went upstairs.

I found the bedroom she'd mentioned and saw the clothes she'd laid out on the bed. Whoever had left this stuff here was shorter than me but fatter, too, so I'd be able to wear it even if the arms and legs were too short.

The bathroom was down the hall. I closed the door behind me and looked around, seeing towels folded up on a shelf and shampoo and soap in the shower. Inside the medicine cabinet I found a new toothbrush still wrapped in plastic and a tube of toothpaste.

Thank God for that. I didn't want to go another minute with my mouth tasting the way it did.

I brushed my teeth until all I could taste was mint. Then I shed my gross-smelling clothes, kicked them into a corner, and turned on the shower.

The house was starting to warm up, but it still felt good to step under the hot spray. I just stood there under the water for a few minutes before I soaped myself up, and by the time I'd rinsed off and stepped onto the bathmat I was feeling more human than I had in days.

I was also feeling hungry. Please, I thought as I went back downstairs, let Claire have ignored what I said. Let there be something to eat.

There was. There were two bows of steaming beef stew and a plateful of cheese and crackers on the kitchen table.

Claire stood behind one of the chairs, looking uncomfortable. "I thought you might be hungry after all," she said.

"I am," I told her, taking the other seat. "I'm starving. Thank you."

"The stew is from cans," she said as she sat down, too.

"It smells great." I took a bite. "It tastes great, too."

We ate in silence, but it wasn't awkward. It wasn't friendly, exactly, but it wasn't unfriendly either. It was sort of . . . neutral, I guess. Thoughtful.

When I was finished I brought my dishes to the sink and started to wash them.

"I can do that," Claire said, coming up behind me.

I shook my head. "You cooked. That means I clean up."

Claire grabbed a dish towel from a hook on the wall and started to dry and put away the dishes I set in the drain. "This is nice of you, but I don't think the normal rules of etiquette apply here. I mean, I did sort of kidnap you."

I smiled down at the glass I was rinsing. "Yeah, you did. But I'm starting to get over it."

"You are?"

"A little. You're not off the hook, though."

"Fair enough."

We finished in silence and then went out to the living room. Claire sat down on the couch while I stayed standing.

"I think I'm going to go to bed," I said.

Claire looked a little disappointed, but she nodded. "Okay."

I sighed. "You wanted to talk, didn't you? You wanted to counsel me and toss out some more medical facts."

One corner of her mouth lifted. "No medical facts, I promise. I did want to talk, but . . ." She paused. "It can wait until tomorrow."

I sat down in the armchair and stretched my legs out toward the fire. "No, go ahead. You won't be able to sleep if you don't get whatever it is off your chest."

Now her whole mouth was smiling. "It's not like that. There's nothing in particular I wanted to say. I just thought, if you felt like it, you could talk about football."

I'd been feeling relaxed, almost mellow. Now I felt my stomach muscles tense.

"Why would I want to do that?"

"I just . . . I don't know. I want to understand why football means so much to you. I mean, I know how popular the game is. I can understand the appeal. It's exciting and even kind of beautiful, in a way. I loved watching your games and I loved watching you play. But you have to admit there are a lot of negatives. Don't you?"

I settled back into the chair. "Like what?"

She leaned forward, her hands on her knees. "It's so violent. Isn't that a problem for you?"

I shook my head. "That's one of the reasons I love football."

She stared at me. "You love the violence?"

I wasn't sure I could explain it to someone who didn't play the game. "I love football because it's rough. Because it's hard. Because it tests your—" I hesitated.

"Masculinity?"

"No. It tests your courage. Your grit. You have to be able to take a hit and get back up again."

"Take a hit? That's how you got a concussion. How can that be a good thing?"

"It's the getting back up that's the good thing." I felt frustrated, knowing I wasn't expressing myself in a way she could understand. "It's like being on a battlefield. Every second of the game is a fight. And it's hard, and a lot of times you want to give up. But every time you don't you get a little stronger."

I expected Claire to argue with me again, but she didn't. She just looked at me, her head tilted to the side and that furrow between her brows that meant she was pondering what she was hearing.

I went on. "I wish you could see us before the game. When we put on all our gear, all the pads and everything, it's like we're strapping on armor. And we know we're going on that field to hit and get hit, and that thousands of people will be watching. Sometimes guys get so tense they throw up in the locker room."

Claire's eyes got wider. "I never saw you look nervous before a game. I've never even heard you talk about being nervous."

I shrugged. "That's because we don't show it to any-one but each other." I took a breath. "That's another thing I've lost because of this stupid concussion. I've lost the team."

"Your teammates still care about you, Will. That's why we're here right now."

"It's not the same thing. Teammates bleed together on the field. I'll never get to do that again."

Claire was quiet for a moment. "It won't be the same, but I could slap you across the face or something."

For the first time in a while, I actually laughed. "Thanks for the offer." I paused. "You don't really get what I'm talking about, do you?"

"I'm not an athlete, so I'll probably never understand that part of it. But I'm in a band, and I'd do anything for my band mates. And even though I've never thrown up I get pretty nervous before I perform. So I understand a little of what you're talking about. I mean, if I had to give up music, I might do exactly what you're doing."

I thought about that. "No, you wouldn't."

"How do you know?"

"Because you're going to be a doctor. You have a lot of other things in your life."

"But so do you! My God, Will, you were on the Dean's list last year. You're smart and funny and sweet and, like, a million other things. I know you talked about going pro but you must've had a backup plan. You always said the NFL was a long shot."

"I know it was a long shot," I said after a moment. "But I was going after it. It's what I wanted more than anything." I dragged my hands through my hair. "Maybe I should've had a backup plan, but I didn't. I don't. I haven't even picked a major yet."

"Will—"

Anger started to bubble up inside me again. "Just stop it, okay? Stop trying to pep me up or whatever. I don't even know why you're wasting your time. I've been an asshole to you."

Admitting that out loud made me remember the day Claire had come over and asked what she could do to help.

You could sleep with me, I suppose. I could stand to burn off a little steam.

It was the shittiest thing I'd ever said to her. To anyone, really. And I'd said it to the girl I'd had a crush on for a year, the girl who'd never been anything but amazing to me.

"You've been going through a lot," she said now.

I couldn't stand for her to defend me anymore. "I wish you'd leave me alone. I'm not worth all this trouble. Believe me. I don't know why you're doing this."

Claire chewed on her lower lip for a second, which was already chapped from the dry air.

"You know what Lou Holtz says?" she said finally. "He says that people need love and understanding and support the most when they deserve it the least."

I stared at her. "You're quoting a Notre Dame football coach to me?"

"Yes, I am. So take me seriously."

I shook my head. "Okay, you win the night. Now I'm going to bed."

She sighed. "All right. I guess I will, too."

As she got to her feet she pulled her phone out of her pocket. "It's a text from Rikki." She read it quickly before looking up again, the furrow back between her brows. "The snow isn't going to stop until tomorrow night. They're not going to drive out until Thursday, but they say they'll come first thing in the morning. Tamsin already bought a turkey."

I sighed. "So I'm trapped here with the woman who kidnapped me, is that what you're saying? For, like, two more days?"

She nodded. "I'm sorry. This didn't work out exactly like I planned, but . . . well . . . I'm still glad I did it."

She looked so earnest and adorable that my heart did that thing it always used to around Claire.

But everything was different now. Back in October, I had something to offer her. I had a skill, a talent, something I was good at. Something I hoped might even lead to gainful employment.

Now I had nothing.

"I can't exactly say the same," I said lightly, "but I'm not as mad at you as I was."

"Well, I suppose that's a start."

The fire had died, but I made sure it was out completely before I headed toward the stairs. Claire followed at first, but when I was halfway up I realized she wasn't with me anymore.

I stopped and turned, my hand on the banister. She was standing at the bottom of the staircase looking up at me.

"What's up?" I asked.

"I think I'm going to stay downstairs for a while," she said. "I want to check the furnace."

I started back down. "I'll do that for you."

She shook her head. "No, I'll be fine. Really." She made a shooing gesture. "Go to bed."

"Well . . . okay. Good night, Claire."

"Good night."

CHAPTER SEVENTEEN

When I woke up the next morning, I had absolutely no idea where I was.

It was the aches and pains in my body that brought my memory back. Every muscle felt stiff, and I knew it was because of my white-knuckled drive from Hart to here—a snowed-in cabin in the middle of the wilderness.

Okay, maybe it wasn't the actual wilderness. We were in western Massachusetts, not the Yukon.

But still. When I looked out my bedroom window, all I could see was falling snow—and through that white veil, trees and hilltops and gray sky.

Even though the house was toasty warm by now—I'd set the thermostat to an indulgent seventy degrees—I shivered. We were so alone out here, cut off from civilization and trapped by the snow. I didn't even know if there was another house within walking distance. I hadn't noticed any lights last night.

All alone . . . except for the very sexy former football player asleep in the next room.

The night before, when Will had started up the stairs on his way to bed, I'd stopped in my tracks to stare at him.

His borrowed pajamas, three inches too short, should have made him look ridiculous. But while the clothes might have been silly, Will himself wasn't.

Something about the snowstorm outside, the fire inside, and the relief of finally getting Will to open up to me seemed to coalesce into a bright warmth inside my belly as I stared up at him. Instead of his too-short pajamas all I saw was the man who wore them, strong and powerful on the outside and hurting on the inside.

I knew if I followed him upstairs I'd keep going right into his bedroom, where I'd tear those pajamas off of him.

But that was the last thing I should do on this . . . trip? Vacation? Kidnapping? Intervention?

Whatever it was, it was about helping Will—not screwing him.

If I acted on my attraction it would be selfish. Will needed a friend now, and that's what I would be.

But oh, how I wished the rest of our friends were here with us. It would be a lot easier to resist temptation if we had some company.

I checked my phone and saw that it was nine o'clock—later than I usually slept but not surprising under the circumstances. I threw off my covers and got out of bed, and on my way to the bathroom I checked on Will.

His door was ajar or I wouldn't have looked in. But it was ajar and I did look in, standing there for at least a minute just watching him sleep.

He was on his stomach with his arms flung out wide. He'd taken off the pajama top before bed, and his upper body was bare. Seeing the thick bands of muscle on his shoulders and back reminded me of the time I'd patched him up after his season opener, and I felt a pang of regret that I'd never see him play another football game.

I still couldn't imagine how much regret Will was feeling.

I backed slowly out of his doorway and headed downstairs. This trip was about helping Will move on, right? So maybe it was time to start strategizing.

I made some coffee and sat down with my tablet to do some research. After an hour or so I got restless, wanting to process what I'd been reading and thinking about. I put on my jacket and a wool hat I found in a bin of outdoor gear beside the door, and then I went out for a walk.

The snow was falling steadily but the wind had died down. The world was utterly, almost mysteriously peaceful. I walked around the house at first, not wanting to go too far, but after a while I wandered into a grove of fir trees.

The scent of pine mingled with the clean scent of the snow. I tilted my head back and closed my eyes, letting the soft flakes kiss my upturned face.

"Hey."

I was so startled I almost fell over.

"Will! Damn it, you scared me to death."

He was standing a few feet away, wearing a navy blue pea coat he must have found in the cabin.

"You? What about me? I woke up and you were gone. As far as I knew you'd gotten lost in the blizzard."

"It's not a blizzard anymore. There isn't a breath of wind." I moved closer and took him by the arm. "Listen."

He looked at me with his eyebrows up. "To what? I don't hear anything."

"Listen harder. It's so still you can actually hear the snowflakes landing. I've never heard such a soft sound before. It's incredible."

He stood there for a moment and then shook his head. "I don't think I—"

"Listen."

This time he was quiet for longer, and I knew the exact moment he heard what I did.

He went absolutely still, like me. And then the two of us stood there, listening to the featherfall of snow on snow. The barest whisper of sound.

It made the silence more profound.

We stood there for a long time. Then I said, "The first time my dad and I met Jenna, she did something I've never forgotten. She teaches music, and she told us her secret for getting a crowd of kids to quiet down and pay attention was a Tibetan bell. She would strike it, and then tell the kids to raise their hands when the last—the very last—vibration of sound faded away. She demonstrated with my dad and me, and then she told us we'd just experienced real silence. The kind of silence that gets into your bones."

Will let out a long breath, and I watched it turn to fog on the cold air. "That was real silence, then." He looked down at me again, and suddenly he frowned. "You're not wearing gloves. They had some in that bin."

I looked down at my hands, which were red and chapped with cold. "I didn't think about it. It's fine, though. I—"

Will pulled off the mittens he'd taken from the bin and held them out. "Here."

"No, that's—"

He didn't wait for me to finish the sentence; he just grabbed my hands and slid the mittens on. "There you go."

I looked down at my now mittened hands, hoping Will couldn't tell that my body was prickling with goose bumps. "Thanks."

Silence fell, but it was different this time. Before, my attention had been on the world around us—the trees, the sky above, the falling snow. Now, all I could focus on was Will.

I'd never known anyone more likely to do a small kindness—or a big one—for someone else. I loved all his contrasts and contradictions: that he'd sacrificed his body to the roughest, most violent sport imaginable and at the same time was the sweetest person I'd ever met.

"Do you want to walk around a little, or are you ready to go back?"

I had to think for a moment before I could answer. "I guess go back? It's probably lunchtime by now."

Right as I said that Will's stomach growled, and he grinned down at me. "I guess you're right. Okay, let's go."

We trudged through the snow—well over a foot of it by now—and back to the cabin.

When we reached the door Will bumped my shoulder with his arm. "Hey, Claire? Thanks."

I wasn't sure what he was thanking me for, but it didn't matter.

"You're welcome."

* * *

We found a frozen chicken pot pie in the freezer and popped that in the oven for lunch. Things between us seemed so friendly, and Will seemed so much like the guy he'd been before his concussion, that I decided to launch into my sales pitch for his future once we finished eating.

After we washed the dishes, I dried my hands on a paper towel and leaned back against the sink. "Okay, so. Can I show you some stuff I looked up?"

Will shrugged. "As long as it's not medical information about CTE or TBI or—"

"It's not."

"Then sure."

We went into the living room, and while I pulled up some of the sites I'd bookmarked on my tablet Will built a new fire in the fireplace. Once he had it going he joined me on the couch, and I tried to focus on what I wanted to talk to him about and not the fact that his leg was only inches from mine.

"All right. You know how you said you don't have a backup plan?"

Will frowned. "I don't—"

"Just listen for a minute, okay?" I turned the tablet so he could see it. "Here are just a few of the things you could do with your football experience." I clicked on each website in turn. "You could be a coach like your stepdad. You could go into sports medicine or sports psychology. You could be a sports writer. If you study business, you could be a marketer for a professional team or a program coordinator for an organization like the YMCA. If you—"

"Claire!"

I stopped talking, staring at Will with my mouth open.

He looked frustrated. No, more than frustrated.

Angry.

"What is it?" I asked defensively. "What did I do wrong?"

He pushed himself to his feet and started pacing back and forth between the couch and the fireplace.

"I may be broken right now but I don't need you to fix me. Jesus, Claire. I thought you dragged me out here to make me feel better, not worse."

"That's what I'm trying to do!"

"By acting like my mother? I already have a mother. I don't need another one."

"Then what *do* you need?"

Asking that made me remember that day at his house, when I'd asked him what I could do to help.

You could sleep with me, I suppose. I could stand to burn off a little steam.

My face flushed red and I had to look away. I knew Will wouldn't ask that now, but in spite of myself, I couldn't help wondering what I'd say if he did.

Maybe I'd answer his snark with the truth.

I've wanted to sleep with you since freshman year.

"What is it? What are you thinking right now?"

My head jerked up and I stared at him. He was standing a few feet away, his arms folded and a scowl on his face.

Well, what the hell. Why not go for truth? This trip was supposed to be about helping Will, not screwing him . . . but I wasn't having much luck with the first thing.

"I was thinking that I want to sleep with you."

I'd never managed to stun someone with my words before. Will's head jerked back like he'd been sucker punched. He actually backed up a couple steps.

"What?"

I wasn't going to say it again. "You heard me."

"Why the hell would you say something like that?"

"Because nothing else I've said has done any good. And because it's true."

Will turned his back on me to face the fire, running both hands through his hair. I sat still and watched him, looking at the bare skin above his shirt collar and thinking that I'd like to kiss him right there . . . and knowing it would never happen.

Finally he turned around again, going over to sit on one of the armchairs. His face was less angry than before, but he didn't look happy, either. "These are the moments I know the universe hates me," he muttered.

"You think the universe hates you?"

He met my eyes. "Why couldn't you have said this a month ago? When you knew I wanted you, and when I actually had something to offer you?"

I was the one getting angry, now. "What, your football studliness? That's not what I—I mean, that's never been the best thing about you. You're a good person, Will. *That's* the best thing about you."

His mouth twisted. "So you're saying I'm a nice guy?"

"Yes. And that's—"

"Did it ever occur to you I might be sick of being a nice guy? I've been a nice guy all my life. Responsible. Considerate. Whatever." He took a deep breath. "Well, I'm done. I want to be the fucked-up guy. I want to be the asshole who skips classes and drinks too much and sleeps with a girl once and breaks her heart."

My worry and frustration and anger and desire swirled together inside me and brought me to my feet.

"So be that guy, then. Sleep with me once and break my heart."

Will stared at me, his jaw tight and something I couldn't decipher in his eyes. "I wouldn't do that to you. Especially not right now. You're just throwing yourself at me like you'd throw a bone to a dog, to calm him down and shut him up."

"That's not true."

"You're trying to patch me up like you did after my game that time. Kidnapping me didn't work and words didn't work and so now you're trying this."

Was it true?

Maybe.

But I didn't care.

"Why do you think that?"

He looked away again. "Because you didn't want me when I was worth something."

It was my turn to pace. "God, you really are an idiot. I've wanted you for a year and a half."

Will looked back at me, and I stopped pacing. "You have?"

I nodded. "But last year I was with someone and this year I didn't want to be. I wasn't ready for a relationship and it seemed like you were, and that's not a good situation. But now you're obviously not ready for a relationship. So I can sleep with you without worrying that you might want more."

His face relaxed a little. "Very funny."

I went right up to his chair and stood in front of him. "You think I'm joking? I've been fantasizing about you for months. I want you, Will. You're the one who doesn't want me."

His whole face looked taut. "You know that's not true."

"So take me, then. Break my heart. Do all the damage you can. I promise you I'm strong enough to put myself back together again."

I couldn't believe I was saying these things. Who the hell was this girl, anyway? I'd never talked to a guy like this in my life—and I was pretty sure I never would again.

I saw emotion chase emotion across Will's face, and I prayed that desire would win. Because there was desire there. I saw it. The same raw, fierce hunger that I felt.

But then his face seemed to shutter and he lurched to his feet, pushing past me and heading for the stairs.

"Running away?" I said to his back. "Wow. You're a lot of things, but I never thought you were a coward."

He stopped at the bottom of the staircase, turning to face me with one hand on the banister. "I'm not going to let you do something you'll regret."

And then I lost my mind. That's the only explanation for what I did next.

"So fucking noble," I sneered, walking toward him. "What happened to not being a nice guy anymore? I guess that was all talk, huh?"

Will squeezed the banister so hard his knuckles turned white. "Stop it."

I kept going until I was less than a foot away from him. "Why should I?"

He was breathing hard. "I'm not going to hurt you."

"You won't. But I don't think that's what you're scared of. I think you're scared that if we sleep together, *you'll* be hurt. You know your whole I-don't-give-a-shit attitude is hollow, and you're afraid that spending the night with me would shatter it."

His jaw hardened. "You must think a lot of yourself. I could sleep with you without giving a shit, Claire. Believe me."

I shook my head. "I don't believe you. If it's true then do it. Kiss me. Fuck me. Do whatever you—"

He grabbed me by the shoulders and pushed me back against the wall. I stared at him, seared by the heat in his green eyes, and then his hands were in my hair and his mouth was on mine and the world fell away.

CHAPTER EIGHTEEN

My heart thundered so hard my body shook with it. I grabbed handfuls of his shirt, desperate to bring him closer.

The whole universe was lips and tongue and teeth and the scrape of stubble on my skin. He tasted like chicken pot pie and coffee and wood smoke, and I didn't want to taste anything else for the rest of my life.

Heat took over. The heat of our mouths, our tongues. The heat where our bodies touched. The heat of Will's hands, his breath, the erection pressed against my stomach. The heat between my legs.

His hands moved from my hair to my shoulders and back again. I felt the frantic urgency in his movements and recognized it.

Because I felt the same thing.

I managed to drag my mouth from his. "Upstairs," I panted.

Will's eyes were wild and his face was flushed. "Are you sure?"

"Upstairs, upstairs, upstairs."

For a moment he looked like he was struggling with himself. Then the struggle was over, and all I saw was the hunger in his face that echoed mine.

"Okay," he said, grabbing my hand and pulling me up the staircase with him.

I tripped halfway and went down on one knee. Will's hand tightened around mine as he started to help me up, but then he stopped.

"What's wrong?" I asked, still sprawled forward with my free hand on the stair above me.

His eyes burned into mine, and I froze.

"Claire," he whispered, and then he was down on the stairs with me, his body on mine and his hands cradling my head.

When our mouths touched my whole body ignited. We were in the most awkward position imaginable, sprawled out on the stairs kissing frantically and desperately, but I never wanted to move. I never wanted to feel anything but this glorious helplessness, this sweet absurdity, this all-consuming fever.

His stubble was scraping my skin and I didn't care. The stairs were digging into my back and I didn't care. The only thing that mattered was his body over mine, his mouth on mine, his tongue tangled with mine until all I could taste was Will.

But when he broke the kiss and started to unbutton my flannel shirt, I stopped him.

"We can do this on a bed," I panted. "There are, like, a bunch of them upstairs."

He stopped unbuttoning and gripped my shirt in his hands, pressing his forehead to mine.

"I'm afraid you'll change your mind," he said, his voice shaking. "I'm afraid you'll come to your senses in an actual bedroom with an actual bed."

My heart thumped painfully in my chest.

"I won't," I whispered. "I promise. Oh, God, Will—I'm not going to change my mind."

He pulled back and looked down at me. "Okay," he said, and then he scrambled to his feet and pulled me up after him, and we stumbled the rest of the way to his room.

Once we were over the threshold he scooped me up in his arms and tossed me onto the bed.

"Why did you do that?" I asked breathlessly, watching as he kicked off his shoes and pulled off his shirt and joined me on the bed in nothing but his jeans.

I was lying on my right side and he was on his left, facing me.

"I want to show you that I'm still strong and manly even though I've lost my football studliness."

I knew he was joking, but I answered him seriously. "You're the manliest guy I've ever known. And the strongest."

His eyes turned bright and patches of red appeared on his cheekbones.

"Claire," he said.

"What?"

His shook his head. "I don't know. I don't know how to say what I'm feeling."

I slid my arms around his neck. "Don't say anything, then."

When we kissed this time it was less frantic and more intense. It was still snowing outside and the sky was dark gray, and the light that came through the two dormer windows was dim. The room seemed to contain a deep kind of privacy, the kind of privacy where two people can come together in ways they don't have words for.

Somehow in the midst of the kissing we managed to get our clothes off, and then we were touching skin to skin. Will was like a human electric blanket I wanted to burrow into forever. And yet in the midst of all that warmth my skin prickled with goose bumps. When he kissed his way down my body his stubble scraped my breasts, and I quivered from head to toe with chills and electricity.

I'd only had sex with one guy before, but I knew I was ready to have sex with Will. There was absolutely no question about it.

But there was a question about something else.

I pulled away from Will and put my hands on his bare chest.

"Condom."

Will's eyes were hooded and hot, and it took a moment for him to come out of the making-out haze.

"What?"

"We don't have a condom. I mean, that was the last thing I thought about bringing on this trip. And I brought you here straight from the bar, so—"

"I have a condom."

I blinked. "What?"

He looked embarrassed. "I put one in my wallet before I went to the bar. I told you I wanted to hook up last night." He paused. "Do you think I'm an asshole?"

"For wanting to have safe sex? No, I don't."

"Not for that. For wanting a hookup."

I shook my head. "You wouldn't have gone through with it. I'm not saying there's anything wrong with hooking up—just that you wouldn't have done it."

He looked almost indignant. "Sure I would. I decided yesterday I was going to fuck my way through life like Delford does."

I grinned at him. "And I'm going back in time to marry Jimi Hendrix. Because there's just as much chance of that happening."

He rolled me onto my back and pressed me down into the mattress, his body on mine from chest to toes and his arms on either side of my head. "You think I can't have casual sex?"

And suddenly my sweet sexy Will was seductive sexy Will, his eyes wicked and his mouth almost but not quite smiling and his hard-on pressing against my bare flesh and making every cell in my body ache for him.

I closed my eyes. "I think you can have a one-night stand," I said. "That's what we're doing, after all. But I don't think it'll be casual."

He flexed his hips just a little bit, and the place between my legs got hot and wet and restless.

He leaned down and spoke right into my ear. "Okay, you've got me there."

And then he pushed himself up and rolled out of bed, and I opened my eyes to see him going over to the bureau where he'd put his wallet.

"Condom," he said, pulling it out and holding it up.

"I never thought anything made of latex could be so beautiful," I said.

He grinned the sexiest grin I've ever seen in my life.

The blankets were all tangled up and pushed down to the foot of the bed, but I'd pulled the sheet up to cover myself after Will got up.

"You're so comfortable," I murmured as he came back toward me.

He lay down on his side facing me, running his hand through my hair as though he loved the way it felt against his fingers.

"Comfortable with what?"

"Yourself. Your body. Being naked."

"My life may have turned to shit, but I know I'm in shape. Although not for much longer if I keep blowing off my workout schedule."

He looked at the sheet covering me and ran a hand along my side, tracing the curve of my torso down to the dip at my waist and back up for the swell of my hip. "You've got to know you have an amazing body, right?"

I shook my head. "I don't hate the way I look or anything, but there are a lot of things I'm insecure about."

He stared at me like I was nuts. "What are you talking about?"

It probably wasn't super sexy to talk about this, but what the hell. "I don't like the shape of my butt."

His eyebrows went up to his hairline. "This here?" he asked, cupping my ass in his hand and making me giggle. "You're kidding me, right? Your butt is perfect."

I shook my head. "You know who has a perfect butt? Julia. She's a dancer and her whole body is perfect. I feel like my hips are too big. My thighs, too. But then my arms are too skinny, and—"

He moved his hand from my backside to cover my mouth. "Stop it. Seriously. I've obsessed over your body so much I could sculpt you from memory. I could make a statue of you like Sam did of Rikki last year. I love every inch of your body. I've dreamed about being with you like this for so long. And now that I'm actually seeing you naked, it's so much better than I thought it would be."

I felt myself blushing. "I'm sorry. I didn't mean to fish for compliments."

"I have a year and a half of compliments stored up for you. I couldn't say you were gorgeous while you were with Ted, and after you broke up . . ." He trailed off.

"After we broke up?"

He didn't answer. Instead he leaned in and kissed me on the mouth. "Hey, Claire?"

"Yes?"

"We stopped making out and started talking. Which is absolutely okay, but it makes me wonder."

"Wonder what?"

"If maybe you're having second thoughts."

I started to say no, but then I forced myself to think about it. We *had* stopped making out. Was there a reason for that? I wanted him as much as ever . . . maybe more. So what was it? Was I having second thoughts?

My eyes moved from Will's face down his perfect body.

His perfect body . . .

And then I knew why I was hesitating.

"It's not that," I said. "I just . . ." I bit my lip. Admitting this would be even less sexy than admitting my physical insecurities, and might even kill the mood between us for good. But we'd gotten this far by being honest and I didn't want to stop now.

I took a breath. "I've only ever been with Ted, and we never burned up the sheets or anything. I mean, I enjoyed being with him, especially in the beginning, but I've wondered sometimes . . . of course Ted would never say it out loud . . . but I've wondered if, maybe, I'm not very good in bed."

Will started to say something and stopped.

"What?" I asked.

He shook his head. "I was about to tell you how ridiculous you're being. But the truth is, I've worried about the same thing. I've only ever been with Lissa and after hearing some of the guys on the team talk . . . well, let's just say I think some of them could give you a better time in bed than I could."

"But I only want to be with you," I said—and then realized how that might sound. "I mean, for this one-night stand thing we're doing."

"I know what you meant," he said. "I feel the same way." He paused. "So then I guess it doesn't matter, right? If you want to be with the person you're with, then whatever happens is what's supposed to happen. Sorry. Does that sound too much like a Zen poster?"

I couldn't remember ever liking someone as much as I liked Will just then. "No. I know exactly what you mean. But, um, we have kind of drifted out of sex terri-tory and into talking territory. Maybe we should just—"

But Will didn't let me finish that sentence. He pulled the sheet off my body, rolled me onto my back again, and kissed me like it was the last thing he'd ever do.

And just like that, the madness returned.

My body blazed to life under Will's. He took me from zero to sixty in the blink of an eye, and before I knew it I was wrapping my legs around his waist and clawing at his back with my fingernails.

He broke the kiss long enough to reach for the con-dom he'd put on the nightstand. He tore the foil cover with his teeth and rose up to his knees to slide the latex on. He was flushed and breathing hard, and he looked exactly like I felt.

"We've got all night, right?" he asked.

"Yes, but why—"

"I feel like we should do more foreplay than this. And I want to, but . . . fuck, Claire, I want to be inside you so much right now. If I know we can do other stuff later, then I—"

I reached up and grabbed him by the shoulders. "Please," I said. "Please."

It was all I could articulate at that moment, but it seemed to be enough.

He kissed me again, hard, and then he reared back as he positioned himself at my center.

When he slid inside me I wanted to die.

I mean it. I wanted to die right then, because I knew that nothing else I could ever experience would be as perfect as that moment.

And then it got better.

Will started to move, slowly at first and then faster and harder. And as he drove himself into me over and over his face filled with a kind of taut bliss I'd never seen before. He closed his eyes, and his jaw was as tight as the bands of muscle over his shoulders.

I couldn't keep my eyes off him. He was so beautiful, so sexy, so—

The tingling started in my fingers and toes, and by the time I knew what was happening an orgasm hit me like a freight train, with a thundering in my ears and a tidal wave of ecstasy.

I gripped Will's arms, and they were as hard as iron as he supported his weight above me.

His eyes were open now, and he was staring down at me like I was the most incredible thing he'd ever seen. "You came," he said, his voice rough and gravelly.

I couldn't speak, but I managed to nod. And then he flexed his hips and thrust in hard, and I felt his body pulse inside me as he came, too.

He collapsed on top of me then, shuddering all over and saying something into the place where my neck met my shoulder.

After a moment I realized it was my name.

"Claire. Claire. Claire."

I could feel the vibration of his voice all through my body. He said my name with reverence, like it was the most important word in the universe.

I wanted to stay like that forever, but after a few minutes I realized that would be impractical.

Breathing was becoming an issue.

I wriggled a little beneath him and he shifted instantly, rolling off and lying on his side facing me. I turned to face him, too, and we gazed at each other in a way that should have been embarrassing.

But it wasn't.

I've never just looked at someone for so long without saying anything. It was like those moments outside in the snow. The silence between us felt like music, somehow—like the spaces between notes had come together to make a symphony.

After a while drowsiness crept over me like a warm blanket. I nestled closer to Will, feeling his arm encircle me as I tucked my head against his broad chest.

And then I was asleep.

When I woke up it was dark. But unlike this morning, I didn't wonder where the heck I was.

I knew exactly where I was.

I took a deep breath and inhaled the scent of Will, deciding I'd rather live on that than air. Then I pressed a kiss to his bare chest, relishing the hardness of that wall of muscle.

"Claire."

Will shifted, tugging me close and kissing the top of my head. After a moment he lifted my chin and kissed me on the mouth.

The kiss was soft and gentle at first. Then, suddenly, it wasn't. Our naked bodies pressed together and we were twisting and writhing and—

Will pulled back.

"What is it?" I gasped, desperate for him.

"I only had one condom."

That calmed me right down. "Oh."

My eyes had adjusted to the darkness and I could see that he was smiling.

"What are you smiling about? Aren't you frustrated?"

"Nope."

"Why not?"

"Because we can do other stuff."

Possibilities opened up before me.

"Other stuff?"

"Other stuff."

And that's what we did.

CHAPTER NINETEEN

When I woke up again, it was daylight.

Bright sun shone through the dormer windows. It came into the bedroom in visible shafts, dust motes dancing in the light.

Suddenly wide awake, I slid out of Will's arms to get out of bed and go over to the window.

The world was blanketed with snow, including my car. But as I stood there, I heard a faint rumble in the distance. I waited, curious, until I saw the source of the noise: a snowplow, making its way down the road past the driveway.

The roads were being cleared. Which was a good thing, because our friends were driving out today.

"Happy Thanksgiving."

I turned and saw Will sitting up in bed, the blankets around his waist and a smile on his face.

My heart warmed at the sight of him. "Happy Thanksgiving."

I was naked, but this morning I didn't feel any self-consciousness about it. How could I, after the way Will had worshiped my body last night?

I padded back to the bed and perched on the edge. "The gang is coming today."

He nodded. "I know." He studied me for a moment, his expression serious. "Can we talk before they get here?"

I didn't pretend not to know what he meant. "About us?"

"Yeah."

"Okay."

We were quiet for a moment. Then Will asked, "Where do we go from here?"

I thought about my answer very carefully, because I wanted to get this right.

"If I were going to be with anyone right now, it would be you. But I'm not ready for a relationship." I paused. "I was with Ted for four years. I was his girl-friend from the time I was fifteen years old. You know how you're not sure who you are without football? I want to be sure I know who I am without being some-one's girlfriend."

I took a deep breath. "I got a single this year because of Ted, you know? So we could have privacy if he came to visit. Then he broke up with me, and I hated having a single. I wished I had a roommate again. But lately . . . the last few weeks . . . I haven't minded it as much. I even kind of like it." I stopped, wondering if I sounded selfish or if Will would know what I meant.

"I get that," he said.

Silence fell between us again, and I waited for Will to speak.

"I wish some things were different," he said finally. "But the fact is, you don't want a relationship right now because you're in a good place, and I shouldn't be in a relationship because I'm in a bad place." He paused. "I guess sometimes people don't sync up. You know? And you shouldn't try to force it."

Even though I knew he was right, and that I'd been right, too, I still felt a sudden unbearable sadness. "We synced up last night," I said. "Like, big time. And maybe next semester . . . or next year . . ."

He took my hand in his. "You don't have to do that," he said. "Let's not look too far ahead, okay?" He raised my hand and kissed it. "Thanks for last night, Claire. It was the best night of my life."

I wanted to say *Me, too,* but I didn't want him to think I was saying it because of what he'd said.

Why is talking so hard sometimes?

He threw off the covers and got out of bed, stretching his arms up to the ceiling. "So I guess we should get ready for visitors, huh? I'll go shovel the driveway."

I got to my feet, too. "I'll help you."

He shook his head. "There's only one shovel," he said. "I saw it yesterday on the back porch. I'll take care of it. It'll be good exercise."

"Well . . . all right."

I stood there for a moment, wondering how to end this conversation and wishing we didn't have to. Because once we did, the magic of last night would be over. And yes, it was the right thing, but I didn't have to like it.

Then I remembered that this was Will's room, which meant that making an exit was up to me.

"So . . . I guess I'll go take a shower. Then I'll make some coffee."

"Sounds good."

I grabbed my clothes from the floor and left.

And that, as they say, was that.

CHAPTER TWENTY

About an hour later, I was finishing up the drive-way when Claire came outside with a shovel in her hand and an indignant look on her face.

"You said there was only one!" she called out, holding up the incriminating evidence in one hand.

I grinned at her. "Yeah, I lied about that."

She started toward me. "Now I'm going to help."

"I appreciate the offer, but there's nothing left for you to do."

She reached my side, looked around, and saw it was true.

"Curse you, McKenna."

"You say the sweetest things."

She looked up at me, squinting with the bright sun-light in her eyes. "I can't believe you did this by yourself."

Staring down into the oceans of blue that were Claire's eyes, I lost my place in the conversation for a moment. Before I had a chance to find it again, we heard the sound of a vehicle coming toward us.

We both turned and listened. It might have been the snowplow coming by again, but I didn't think so. Then, after a minute, a navy blue van came lurching down the dirt road.

"It's one of the Panther team vans," I said.

We backed up the driveway to give them room, and after they pulled in, here came our friends.

Tamsin and Julia and Dyshell. Rikki and Sam. Andre and Tony and two more teammates: Derrick and Isaiah.

My throat felt tight all of a sudden. There was a lump there, and it wasn't easy to talk past.

"Don't you people have families?"

Tamsin grinned up at me, her dark hair hidden under a neon pink knit hat and her arms full of groceries. "We decided we'd rather spend Thanksgiving with you."

"That's some seriously questionable decision making," I said as I reached for the bags.

Andre was holding a big turkey wrapped in plastic. "That's what I told them, but they wouldn't listen. Where's the kitchen? I need to get this thing in the oven if we're going to eat before midnight."

We actually ended up eating around six o'clock.

Okay, so, I've already made it clear that I love my mom and my stepdad. Not only are they awesome parents, but they're good company. Holidays with them are always fun.

So I mean no disrespect when I say that this was the best Thanksgiving I ever had.

It's quite a thing when a bunch of your friends blow off their plans to spend the holiday with you, just because you're having a rough time. It's humbling, not to mention an effective way to get you back on the right track.

And it was Claire who'd made it happen.

I didn't sit next to her during dinner, figuring I'd give myself away for sure if I was within touching distance of her. But my eyes kept drifting to where she was, across the table between Tamsin and Julia.

I really, really hoped that Claire would decide to be with me some day. Because if she didn't, I was going to be single for the rest of my life.

She was it for me. The only girl, forever.

Okay, I know that sounds melodramatic coming from a nineteen-year-old. But I never felt that way about Lissa, even though I'd loved her and was committed to her.

Was it possible my feelings would change if Claire and I never got together? Sure. But right then, at that moment in my life, I couldn't imagine it.

The food was delicious and the conversation was fun, but the highlight for me was watching Claire. I could never get enough of looking at her, of seeing her smile and laugh with her friends.

Seeing her happy.

Once dinner was over, we all helped with the clean-up. When everything was mostly done and there were just a few dishes left to wash, people started to drift into the living room until it was down to just me and Sam.

I liked Sam a lot but the two of us never hung out together outside of group things. As I washed the last of the glasses and Sam finished putting the dishes in the cabinets, I wondered if there was something I should be asking him about. A particular class? Some kind of sculpture thing he was doing? I knew he liked basketball. Was he on an intramural team?

"Hey, Will?"

I almost dropped the glass I was holding. "Yeah?"

Sam closed the cabinet door and leaned back against the counter, his hands in his jeans pockets. "So, this is none of my business."

Uh oh.

"Yeah?"

"But at dinner, I noticed the way you were looking at Claire."

I stared at him. The fact that Sam and I weren't that close made it worse. If he'd noticed, probably everyone had.

"I don't think anybody else saw what I did," he went on. "But last year when I was losing my mind over Rikki, the face I saw in the mirror was the face you've got now."

I didn't know what to say. Should I deny it? Not for my sake, but for Claire's? I was one hundred percent sure she didn't want anyone to know what we'd done last night, and since she wanted to stay single, I didn't think she'd want me sharing all the details of my feelings or whatever.

Sam went on. "The only reason I'm even saying anything is that the situation with Rikki had me pretty messed up last year. It only got better after I told her how I felt. I know you're having a bad time right now, and if you're into Claire and not telling her, I think that could make things worse. Or at least harder." He shrugged. "For what it's worth."

I frowned down at the floor. After a moment Sam said, "Anyway, I'm sorry if I pissed you off by bringing it up. Like I said, it's none of my business."

He started to head out and I made a decision.

"Hold up," I said.

He turned back. "Yeah?"

"You're not wrong. I am into Claire. But it can't happen right now."

Sam studied me for a second. "You're not happy about that."

"It's not just that. I mean no, I'm not happy about it. But the thing is . . . before all this football shit, I could see us being together when the time was right, you know? And I knew it would be perfect. But now . . ."

I wasn't sure exactly what I was trying to say, but Sam seemed to get it.

"I know what that feels like. If I tell you something about me and Rikki, can you keep it to yourself?"

I nodded.

"We were both virgins when we got to Hart. We went to the same high school, and I'd been in love with her a long time. When we started getting closer last year I thought it was meant to be. Like we were supposed to have our first time together and it would be perfect." He looked rueful. "Then I screwed it up. One night when it seemed like things with Rikki were never going to happen, I hooked up with a girl I didn't even know." He shook his head. "That was my first time. Right after it happened, Rikki and I finally told each other how we felt. She said she was so glad our first time would be with each other."

I knew what was coming next. Everyone knew this part of the story.

"I was planning to tell her the truth, but someone told her before I could. Maybe you know what happened with Jason?"

Jason used to be in Claire's band, and he'd been into Rikki last year. Someone had sent him a pic of Sam with the other girl, and Jason had shown it to Rikki.

I nodded. "Yeah, I know."

"That blew everything up between me and Rikki, and I hated myself for weeks. How could I have done that? Everything could have been so perfect if I hadn't fucked it all up." He paused. "But then I figured out that things don't have to be perfect. If you screw up, it doesn't mean you can't try to fix it. So I did, and Rikki and I got together." A slow smile spread across his face. "We've been together for a year, and it's not perfect. But it's so much better than I ever imagined . . . even though nothing happened like I thought it would."

I thought about what Sam had said for the rest of the night. We were all hanging out in the living room, recovering from the huge dinner we'd eaten. I'd built a fire, and now I was lying on the rug in front of it with my arms behind my head.

The mood was mellow. Claire must have told Andre that the intervention had been successful, because we didn't talk about any of my issues—thank God. The conversation had been all over the map, and a couple of times I'd laughed so hard it hurt.

It felt good to laugh with my friends again.

Tamsin and Julia decided to stay the night here. They would drive back with me and Claire in the morning, while everyone else would go back tonight in the van. It was after eleven o'clock and Andre said something about leaving before midnight, but we were all sprawled around in post-turkey contentment and no one seemed eager to move.

The athletes had zeroed in on the single ladies—Tamsin, Julia, Dyshell, and Claire—and were explaining the differences between the NCAA football and basketball championships. They'd already participated in Tamsin and Dyshell's How Badass is Beyoncé discussion, so they probably felt entitled to a little sports talk.

Claire was sitting on the couch with her legs curled under her, her head resting on Dyshell's shoulder. Her eyes were drifting closed, which meant I could stare at her without worrying that she'd catch me.

The few times our eyes had met at dinner, it had been like fireworks going off in my heart.

Yeah, I had it bad.

Claire might not have it as bad as me, but from the way her cheeks turned red whenever we looked at each other, I knew she was thinking about last night.

I'd done plenty of thinking about that, too. But right now, watching Claire fall asleep, I wasn't thinking about sex.

I was thinking about a future with the girl I loved.

Talking with Sam had shifted something inside me. I no longer felt like I'd ruined everything by getting myself concussed and acting like an asshole for weeks and sleeping with Claire too soon. I realized that I couldn't change anything that had already happened, and that I couldn't control what Claire was thinking or feeling.

Not that I'd ever want to.

But I could control myself, and I could make changes in my own life. Right now, I wasn't the guy Claire deserved. And while I knew I would never be perfect, I could be better.

I wanted to be better.

I realized something else, too, sitting in a roomful of friends who'd sacrificed family plans to spend Thanksgiving with me after I'd blown off my own family.

They were right and I was wrong.

There was more to my life than football. Some things I knew about already; others I still had to figure out.

I scrambled to my feet and went upstairs for a little privacy. Then I called my house.

"Will! I'm so glad you called. Happy Thanksgiving!"

"Happy Thanksgiving, Mom. I'm sorry for calling so late."

"That's all right. Did you get any turkey?"

It was just like her to sound sweet and cheerful and to give me a pass on the way I'd been acting lately . . . and the way I'd been blowing her off.

"Yeah, I did. My friends ended up buying all this food and cooking a huge dinner."

"That sounds lovely. And you had a good time?"

"Yeah. But that's not why I called."

I hesitated for a moment, and my mom didn't rush to fill the silence. That's another thing I love about her.

"So, you know how you said you weren't going to let me get a second opinion or transfer to another school?"

"Yes."

"I just wanted to say I get where you're coming from. I'm thinking about what you said. And . . . I'm sorry for the way I've been acting."

Pause.

"Oh, Will."

"Mom, are you crying? If you are, cut it out. Go get Alex, will you? I need to apologize to him, too."

"I'm walking the phone downstairs now. Oh, Will, I love you so much."

"I know. I love you, too, Mom."

After I hung up with Alex I went back downstairs. People were starting to get ready to go, and Claire was still asleep on the couch.

Dyshell looked up when I walked over. "Would you mind taking over for me as pillow? I need to use the bathroom before we take off."

"Sure," I said, taking Dyshell's place and letting Claire curl up against me.

There was nowhere else on earth I'd rather be.

Claire wanted to be single for a while to focus on herself. I needed to do that, too. I needed some time to figure out the next phase of my life.

And then?

Then we'd see.

I wasn't going to pressure Claire to be with me, but I wasn't going to give up, either. And I was going to be the best damn friend I could, because that's what she deserved—and because I wanted her in my life any way I could have her.

If friendship was what we ended up with, I'd take it and be grateful.

But when the time was right, I'd let Claire know I wanted a hell of a lot more.

CHAPTER TWENTY-ONE

The next few months were pretty good.

I didn't see much of Will in December, but we were both busy with finals. He pulled himself together and aced most of his, which made me really happy. Then, of course, came Christmas and winter break.

During the week between Christmas and New Year, Will and I got into the habit of texting every night. Nothing sexy or even flirtatious—just friend stuff, sometimes funny and sometimes serious.

It was the best part of my day.

When we came back to Hart in January, Will was in a really good place. He enrolled in a journalism class and did a few pieces on college athletics for the Hart Star, and when one of his articles got some national attention, he started talking about being a sports writer.

I was in a good place, too. I liked my classes and my songwriting was going well, and the band was sounding sharper and tighter every day.

"We need an original love song from you," was their only complaint.

We covered some romantic ballads in our regular set list, but I hadn't contributed anything of my own on that theme. I'd written a bunch of angry post-breakup songs, along with a few cynical love sucks-type tunes, but I hadn't ventured into the positive side of romance since before my breakup with Ted.

Well, except for a song I'd been working on since Thanksgiving. A song I had no intention of ever sharing with anyone.

Will and I started hanging out a lot once the new semester started. He was always the person I wanted to share good news with, and the person I wanted to comfort me if I had a shitty day. We still texted every night before bed.

It seemed like we were building towards something— something really good. I started waiting for Will to bring it up, to talk about moving our relationship forward.

But the days went by and nothing happened.

Then it was February, and my dad and Jenna came to Hart for a visit. My dad made dinner reservations and told me to invite a friend, and Will was the one I picked.

He showed up at the restaurant in a jacket and tie.

"What's all this?" I asked, waving my hand at his suit while we followed my dad and Jenna inside.

"I want your folks to like me," he said with a grin.

They didn't like him.

They loved him.

"Claire told us about the article you wrote for your school newspaper," my dad said over dessert. "About college athletes and concussion?"

Will nodded. "Claire helped me with the medical research. She's going to be an amazing doctor."

My dad looked pleased by that. "She said the article was reprinted in student papers around the country."

Will nodded again. "The NCAA is taking a look at their concussion guidelines. I'm going to be part of a student group that will talk to them this spring. I'm not sure what the right answer is to the concussion problem, but I know we have to be asking more questions."

"Well," my dad said. "I think student athletes will have a good advocate in you."

It was the best dinner-with-the-parents ever. Every girl's dream of the perfect first meeting between her boyfriend and her family.

Except, of course, that Will wasn't my boyfriend.

"Are you coming to Boston tomorrow?" Jenna asked. "To see Claire's band?"

That was the reason my dad and Jenna were in town. The Red Mollies were doing an east coast tour, and they were playing a Boston club tomorrow night.

Sugar Lane was opening for them.

It was our biggest gig ever. My dad was going to be there, and most of my Bracton friends—including Will.

"I wouldn't miss it," he said now. "I love seeing Claire perform. She's electric."

Now it was Jenna's turn to look pleased. "Yes, she is."

I was starting to feel embarrassed. "I'm not electric."

Will frowned. "Are you kidding?"

I shrugged. "Even if I am, that's just my musical persona or whatever. It's easy to be all kickass when it's just an act."

Jenna started to say something, but Will got there first.

"Or maybe that's who you really are, and you just need to let yourself be that person in the rest of your life."

There was a short silence. Then:

"*Thank* you," Jenna said to him. "That's what I've been telling her."

Yeah, he hit that dinner out of the park.

"Tell me again why you two aren't dating?" Jenna asked me when we went to the restroom.

I didn't have an answer for her.

The truth was, I'd been waiting for Will to make a move. To say, *The time has come. Let us be boyfriend and girlfriend and ride off into the sunset.*

But he didn't.

I started to worry that our window of opportunity had closed. I'd felt good about my decision to stay single last semester, but now that Will was doing so great and I felt ready to be part of a couple—to be with Will—I wasn't sure he felt the same way anymore.

Of course that had been the risk all along. Sometimes people don't sync up, Will had said.

Maybe we would never sync up. Maybe we were meant to stay friends.

But every time I thought that, Will would touch me. He'd bump my shoulder or give me a hug, and my knees would turn to jelly.

That is not the response of a friend.

Okay, so, maybe I should make the move. I mean, I'd been the one to put the brakes on at Thanksgiving, right?

I'd thought about all the ways I could do it. I could just grab him and kiss him, of course. I could ask him out on a date or something formal like that. Or . . .

Or nothing.

The more I thought about it, the more nervous I felt. What if Will didn't feel the same way anymore? What if he didn't want things to change? If I fucked this up, the stakes were really high.

I'd lose my best friend.

The more time went by, the less willing I felt to take responsibility for that.

It would be much better to wait for Will to make the move. That way, it wouldn't be my fault if everything got messed up.

* * *

Jocelyn had a van, which made her Sugar Lane's de facto transport. After we got the instruments stowed inside we had room for one more, so Tamsin traveled with the band to Boston the next day.

The two of us sat in the back together. Tamsin showed me the tattoo she'd gotten last week—a red heart on her ankle.

"I really like it," I said. "Maybe I'll get one, too. I feel like I should have tattoos, you know? I'm supposed to be a musician."

"You *are* a musician," Tamsin corrected me. She paused. "So, it's February."

"That is undeniably true."

"The Semester of Us is officially over."

"It's been over for two months."

"Yes, it has. Are you ready to fall off the wagon?"

I thought about it. "Are you?"

"Nope."

I stared at her. "Seriously?"

"Seriously. I'm thinking about a Year of Us. Or at least a Year of Me," she added. "I mean, I don't expect you to stay single and celibate your entire sophomore year." She grinned. "Especially since, if you'll excuse my mentioning it, Will McKenna is about as crazy in love with you as any guy I've ever seen."

Just like that, goose bumps swept over my entire body.

"I think I'm in love with him, too," I whispered.

"Yeah. That's pretty fucking obvious."

I stuck my tongue out at her.

"So why the hell aren't you doing anything about it?" she asked.

I sighed. "Because I'm scared?"

"Sure. But do you think you're going to be any less scared tomorrow? Or next week, or next month, or—"

"Okay," I said, stopping her. "I get it."

"I'm just saying. Life is short and whatnot."

"That's very profound."

"I'm a fountain of profundity." She paused and looked out the back window. "Hey, we're here! Are you guys ready for the big time?"

* * *

It turns out there isn't enough deodorant in the world to prepare you for your band's first major gig.

But once we got through our first song, I knew it was going to be okay.

Part of that was seeing all our friends in the audience. Rikki and Sam, Julia and Dyshell, Izzy and Mena and what looked like every resident of Bracton—along with the entire Panthers football team.

Among the other reasons for Sugar Lane to feel proud tonight, we could now claim credit for bringing the art geeks and the athletes of Hart University together in one place.

Will was there, too. I kept seeing his face in the crowd, and every time I did, my heart glowed brighter and I sang harder.

Then, when we were close to the end of the set, I saw him again. He was dancing like a maniac—with Becky.

I finished that song on autopilot, and the next one, too. I felt like my heart had been sucked out of my body. I managed to get through the rest of the set, but even though the crowd cheered and the band was ecstatic as we left the stage, Jenna knew something was up.

"Are you okay?" she asked me as she was getting ready to go on with the Mollies. "You guys were fantastic, but you seemed a little tense at the end there. Did all the excitement catch up with you?"

"Maybe," I said, using the towel she'd handed me to wipe the sweat from my eyes. "It was awesome, though.

We'll never forget the night we opened for the Red Mollies."

She gave me a quick hug. "I have a feeling the Mollies are going to remember the night they shared a stage with you. Congratulations, kiddo. Sugar Lane rocked the house."

As soon as she took the stage with her band, the crowd erupted. Jocelyn, Milton and Burns went out into the club to be part of it, and I told them I'd join them in a minute.

But I didn't. Instead, I stood in the shadows and watched Will.

He wasn't with Becky anymore. I saw her over by the bar, laughing and dancing with Andre and Dyshell. Will was up front near the stage, in the crush of fans dedicated enough to get that close.

Once the song was over and Jenna was introducing the next one, I saw Will turn and scan the room.

Was he looking for me?

And then, in that moment, I realized something.

I could spend the next week or month or year asking myself questions like that. Was Will looking for me? How did he feel about me now? Did he still want me? Was he interested in someone else?

Or I could take a chance and tell him how I felt.

I went backstage and waited for what Jenna called the "breather" song. That was the one near the middle of the set when each musician had a solo. After she finished her guitar jam, Jenna came off stage to gulp down some water.

That's when I grabbed her.

CHAPTER TWENTY-TWO

The Red Mollies were awesome, but I couldn't fall into the music the way I'd fallen into Claire's set.

Of course if Claire were with me it would be different. I kept looking for her, and even though the club was a madhouse I couldn't understand why I didn't find her.

She'd looked a little stressed out during her last few songs. Was she feeling sick? Should I try to get backstage and look for her?

Then Jenna took the microphone.

"Okay, everybody, we're going to change things up a little. I'd like to invite Claire Stone back onstage to perform a new song. She's never played it in public before, so this is something special for the people here tonight."

The moment Claire came out I forgot everything else. The heat and the people jostling me faded into the background, and the only thing that existed was Claire.

She was nervous, although I didn't think anyone but me would pick up on that. I could tell from the way she held her guitar—a little tighter than usual—and the way she bit her lower lip before she spoke into the microphone.

"Hi, everybody." She paused. "This is a love song. The guy I wrote it for is here tonight, so . . . it seemed like a good time to play it."

That was her whole introduction. She took a deep breath, looked down at her guitar, and started to play.

I heard the music more than the words. It was gorgeous, like everything Claire wrote, but it was more than just a beautiful melody.

A hundred different things were in that song. Her hands on me after the season opener, healing the damage from the game. Tigger and Piglet and the way we could talk about anything. Listening to the falling snow, and the way we could be silent.

The night we'd spent together.

When she was done I didn't even clap, although I was glad everyone else did. Claire left the stage and I just stood there like an idiot, my heart thumping against my ribs, until she found me a few minutes later and pulled me away from the crowd.

"Hey," I said, looking down at her.

"Hey."

I waited a moment, and so did she.

Then I cleared my throat. "So. Was that song about me?"

One side of her mouth quirked up. "Please tell me you already know the answer to that question."

There were a lot of things I could have said—some of them clever, some of them cautious. But what came out was,

"I love you."

Claire's eyes widened. "Oh, Will." There were tears on her lashes, and she blinked them away. "I love you, too." She took a deep breath. "I love you so much."

And then I pulled her into my arms and kissed her.

We were standing in the shadows at the edge of the dance floor, occupying our own little bubble of privacy.

But even if we'd been on stage under a spotlight, I would have done exactly the same thing.

ACKNOWLEDGEMENTS

Thanks as always to Mikel Strom and Tara Gorvine for their help, encouragement, and endless patience, and to my mother for her general awesomeness. Thanks to Sarah Hansen (Okay Creations) for her gorgeous cover, and to the folks at Victory Editing for their eagle eyes. And finally, an epic thank-you to my readers, who are the reason I write.

ABOUT THE AUTHOR

Abigail Strom started writing stories at the age of seven and has never been able to stop. On her way to becoming a full-time writer, she earned a BA in English from Cornell University as well as an MFA in dance from the University of Hawaii, and held a wide variety of jobs from dance teacher and choreographer to human resource manager. Now she works in her pajamas and lives in New England with her family, who are incredibly supportive of the hours she spends hunched over her computer.

For more information, visit her at abigailstrom.com.